True You 101

True You 101

TJ Eckhart

Copyright © 2020 TJ Eckhart.

Cover Design by Suzanne Johnson

Liminal Books
Between the Lines Publishing
410 Caribou Trail
Lutsen, MN 55612
btwnthelines.com

First Published: 2020

Liminal Books is an imprint of Between the Lines Publishing. The Liminal Books name and logo are trademarks of Between the Lines Publishing.

The publisher is not responsible for websites (or their content) that are not owned by the publisher.

ISBN: 978-1-950502-31-8 (paperback)
Printed in the United States

This book is inspired by my partners, myself, my friends, my family, and everyone else who struggled in our teen years because we simply could not fit into the cisgender, heteronormative models that surrounded us. We found the magic inside ourselves to become who we truly are and to find or build the community we need.

We have never been abnormal, and we have never been alone.

Chapter 1: Most Loved, Most Hated

Dear Journal

Most people believe that unless you are a certain age, you won't remember events clearly. Sure, tragedy can leave emotional scars, but details will be fuzzy.

I remember everything about the day my parents failed to come home. It was the most terrifying day of my life.

I'm Blake Trudeau, and I just know that as soon as I step across the classroom threshold, this is going to be the most terrifying year of my life.

My sophomore year of high school

"Welcome, new students!" the professor greets us as we walk into her classroom. Most of us come in pairs, a few in trios; my best friend is already inside sitting in his seat when I look around the door. Sebastianus Hiles' family lives on the same block as mine. We've known each other through his parents and my grandmother and uncle, who must meet regularly with other mages who have chosen to live in the borough of Brooklyn in the mortal world. Seb turns and waves at me, his grin wide.

Of course, he is happy to be here; he isn't hiding a fundamental part of himself like I am.

"Where were you this morning?" I ask him as I take my assigned seat. I know which desk is mine, because it emits a soft-white light that only I can see. I'm a couple rows down from Seb, but class hasn't begun for the day, so I stay standing and frown up at him when he just shrugs his shoulders. "I waited at the bus stop, but you never came," I press.

Seb looks directly at me for a moment; his gaze travels up and down my form, making me uncomfortable. His grayish-blue eyes get a bit wider and a touch dilated. He's been looking at me more intently ever since he got back from his summer vacation two weeks ago. Normally he calms down after a few of my taunts, but today he swallows and looks pointedly away. "I've got to get to campus earlier this semester. I thought I told you that?"

Did he? He told me all about his vacation—my uncle's job, like my parents' used to, keeps us close to the mortal world, so our vacations can't be three months long like the Hiles family summer vacations tend to be. He did mention something, so I ask, "Is this a football thing?" I use the British term for the sport because my grandmother and uncle still use that word.

Now he turns and frowns at me, his gaze directed at mine. "I'm first student manager. I have to be there for practice before most of the players. And it's soccer, not football."

"Oh," I reply. *That's right.* He was complaining about how he hadn't really bulked up over the summer or added more than an inch in height. I think he said he didn't want to be an average white boy any longer. Maybe he feels he doesn't stand out in a crowd—here or out in the mortal realm—but I've always found his thin, straight, light-brown hair interesting. I feel my cheeks heat up and take the approach of more students as an excuse to look away.

I turn back when Seb calls down, "I can still do lunch and the ride home." He adds with another shrug, "If you want."

"Sure," I agree quickly. The students between us giggle but don't comment as I turn and sit down. The professor and her assistant are urging everyone to take a seat, so I get out my ritual case and my personal school journal.

Each journal looks different if you take the time to examine them all. When I entered the Institute last year, mine was white; now it's pale yellow, getting darker with each semester of classes. It also bears my name in a unique script that I wish my hand could make. The magic ink seems to undulate in ever-changing colors. My family's house sigil—a sturdy mountain goat—and the astrological signs for my birthdate complete the cover decorations.

Teachers use the journals to grade homework and track class development, but they can only see the pages that deal with their course. The purple box on one corner of the professor's desk channels magic that sends copies of the proper pages to the individual instructors. The first class of the day gives everyone's journal the box treatment, but not today, not our first day of the term.

Since everything else in the journal can only be read by me, I've been using it as my personal diary. In it I can keep track of my feelings (too many) and physical changes (too few) without fear that someone might invade my privacy or demand access to it. The best thing about coming to magic school has been this journal.

"While every one of you knows your own name, or you should," the professor teases us, "let me introduce you to the two of us, and then we'll get started. I am Dareia Russo. This is my fourteenth year at Reinholdt and my twelfth year of teaching *True You*." I take a good look at the teacher, noting her pale skin; subtle-green eyes that are crinkled up with her smile; and her blondish red hair, which she wears pulled back. As she turns to the man next to her, I see that her hair is quite long, nearly to the small of her back, even though it is braided and falls in a straight line along her spine. She appears to be of average height and weight for most white women, but her form is clearly feminine, unlike my own.

Professor Russo continues, "This is our tutor, Geraint Lubit, who has been helping me for three years now. Contact information for both of us is inside the cover of the textbook you are being handed right now." Tutor Lubit is a good hand taller than the instructor, but he is standing back from her out of respect for their roles, something I noticed last year among all the classes that have teaching assistants. He has darker skin than the professor but is still paler compared to me, though his hair appears to be about as dark and thick as my own. He wears it closely trimmed, like my uncle's. I can't see his eyes well behind his square-framed glasses. I guess this course won't correct vision problems, not that I have to worry about that. Trudeaus have always had great eyesight.

In the mundane world of Collegiate Academy, where everyone in New York City thinks I go to school, Professor Russo's course would be called *Human Sexuality*. Here at the Reinholdt Institute of Sortilege Arts, the course is called *True You 101*. It's the most loved and hated course of the sophomore year.

I look at the textbook, similar to the school journals, because each copy will be blood-bound to one student. The magics we'll be working with can track our progress, our changes, and our reactions on physical, emotional, and mystical levels. However, professors, tutors, and even administration can read it at any time. At the end of the course, the books erase and reset for the next year.

How do I know? I read all the materials my uncle gave me about this place at the end of eighth grade, when Grandmother informed me that I needed to leave the private school in Brooklyn and attend a magic school in Manhattan. My family taught me that the best way to keep a secret from the mortal world is to learn everything about it. I read, watch, and listen to everything I can get my hands on. I study things that not even my family knows about, and certainly not anyone at school. I once thought about telling Seb, but I'm worried that he'll be afraid of me, as I am of myself most days. I'm grateful when the professor speaks up again, because it disrupts this distressing line of thought.

"Now that everyone has a textbook," Professor Russo instructs, "let's perform the personal binding spell that hopefully you all remember from your first day of class last year. Everyone open your ritual kits and get out your knife. We'll do this together." Both she and Tutor Lubit get their kits out to perform the ritual with us, though their targets are class binders and grade books.

I slide the knife along my pinky finger and let a few drops of blood fall onto the cover of the textbook as I recite the phrases with the rest of the class. The book glows for a moment, and then the fancy writing of my name appears in the upper left-hand corner of the cover.

"Excellent work," Professor Russo tells us. "Now we'll turn to the first page, and Tutor Lubit, will you do the honors of reading us the course syllabus?"

"Of course, Professor. Welcome to *True You 101*," he says before beginning to read in a clear, calm—but luckily not monotone—voice. The tutor for *Mage History 101* last year nearly put me to sleep with his dry tones, and some of my early grades showed it.

It takes him ten minutes to read the syllabus, and by the time he's done, all of us have signed our names at the bottom of it, agreeing to the rules and regulations. When I went to mundane school from preschool through eighth grade, we rarely had syllabi, and when we did, most teachers just assumed we'd read or not read it on our own. Everyone told me it was an easy out, because no one could prove anything without the paper syllabus. If you wanted to get out of an assignment or get extra credit, you'd appeal to the teacher or have your parents talk to them.

My grandmother and my uncle refused to intercede on my behalf for academic matters, but when I was bullied, they rushed in. After some girls saw my secret in sixth-grade PE class, I got bullied a lot. My guardians became regulars at PTA and parent-teacher meetings and put in routine appearances at the headmaster's and principal's offices. My uncle's job somehow allowed him to get any online bullying erased as soon as I brought it to his attention—this same mysterious job also permitted us to easily move to the States. Eventually, the bullies got tired and moved to easier targets, but the rest of that school year was a nightmare. My life improved when we moved to NYC and I had a new private mortal school for seventh grade. That's when I started keeping my secret super close.

Grandma and Uncle Delmar have stayed active here at the Institution but haven't needed to make extra visits. I've worked hard to keep my secret safe by using hygiene spells we learned last year, coupled with some of my grandmother's herbal remedies to decrease any sweat I might work up in required physical courses. I've joined a few student groups that focus on arts and speech to build up friendships—ones that value my mind versus my body. I just hope it will be enough to counter the bullying if word spreads about what I am.

The professor walks around looking at every textbook. She touches each with a finger, which then glows white or red depending on the quality of the spell. Mine glows a bright white, and I catch a smile from her when I glance up.

Magical work must be very carefully done, so it is never acceptable to ignore the rules. I've known this since before preschool. I've caught Grandmother and

Uncle having whisper fights about my parents, and the words that have made the biggest impression on me were "against the rules," "poorly executed," and "if you had only planned more thoroughly." I'm not really sure what it all means, but I double- and triple-check everything I do. I don't want to mess up things so badly that I can't return home someday. I know how much that hurt me and Grandmother, and I won't do that to her.

I glance back at Seb, but he's glancing toward Burim Choudhury, who was voted most handsome boy in our class last year for the yearbook. Burim has golden tones to his dark skin, wavy, thick, black hair, and shoulders that are definitely wider than they were last term, along with a good half foot of extra height. His eyes, though, always seem angry to me, so I just can't understand what others see in him. Seb blushes when Burim looks at him with a frown. Seb's blush darkens when he catches me looking at him, so I roll my eyes and turn back to the textbook.

I sigh as I turn to the next page: the table of contents. The class covers the basics first—eye color, hair color and length—the things even a mere mortal could change without much cost or effort. "We start with the simplest topics, so you can understand the magic and learn to adjust to each change," Professor Russo explains when the tutor pauses and looks toward her. I finger the ends of my two braids. It might be nice to have something other than dark-brown, thick, and tightly curled hair.

"Then the class will tackle 'Ancestral Heritage Physicality,' or what you might call race and ethnicity," Tutor Lubit continues at the professor's nod. "Long ago, physical environment affected the types of magical talents and practices mages developed. Mages living in a hot desert environment would have no need to learn about cold magic, just as mages living on the shores of a great ocean had little need to learn agricultural magic—or so our historians believe. But, like mortals, mages generally prefer to associate with others like themselves. Although that tendency can create very powerful mages, it can also cause stagnation, leading to errant or even dangerous talents, so it became common for marriages to be arranged between mages of vastly different environments."

He pauses, and the professor interjects with a smile, "Of course, with the development of portal magic and mortal mass transportation, we don't need to arrange marriages anymore—instead, we encourage our young people to travel and experience different cultures for themselves." Some of the students around me start giggling. The tutor continues about how magic came to the mortal realm, but I just tune it out since we learned this last year.

Through my parents, I was easily three different broad racial groups by mortal standards—White European, Western African, and East Asian. My looks, and the fact that Mom and Dad were together, weren't too shocking back in London, but in America I have gotten a few second glances. This is especially true when I'm with only my grandmother, whose nose is slightly smaller than mine, eyes more almond shaped, and our skin tones significantly different. With my uncle, though, we barely get noticed, because he looks more like me than my parents did.

I push that realization aside and focus on what Tutor Lubit is describing next. "Chapter Three will change our physical form but leave us in our natural ancestry."

I frown for a moment and again the tutor's voice fades as my thoughts whirl. That seems backwards. Wouldn't it be more challenging to be a different race than to just be a bit taller or fatter? I hope I won't be required to go thinner since I'm not the biggest person to begin with—a fact my uncle comments on if I don't seem to be eating enough.

As though reading my worry, Tutor Lubit pauses at this point and says, "Chapter Four can be traumatic, so think of the third as a bit of a break."

"Don't discount the challenges of your body being a bit different," the professor adds before the tutor continues reading. "A few kilos here and there, an inch or two of height lost or gained—it can have a profound impact on many."

The fourth topic makes me press my lips together tightly: *Gender and Sexuality*. This is probably where our class would overlap most with its rough equivalent in the mortal world, except it won't be only theory or empathy we work with. I glance down at my lap, certain that I'm the only one worried about this. I've never known a different body, a different array of private parts, but I hope that when this is all done I can just be a normal girl.

Most people look at me and think I'm a girl—sometimes a tomboy or a princess depending on what I'm doing and what I've decided to wear. At Reinholdt we all have identical blazers, shirts, trousers, and shoes. Only the most obvious physical traits, behavior, or accessories give clues to our gender. All our restrooms are single admittance to cut down on loafing when we should be somewhere more important. In the girls' gym room, we usually just magic ourselves clean and change uniforms without disrobing. That also makes hiding my secret easier, because the tricks I employed in seventh and eighth grade seem normal here.

Most of my classmates have been changing physically since arriving at the Institute last academic year—the girls changing more than the boys at this point. Except me—my changes are subtle, hidden. These months in

True You may clarify what I am, but I'm terrified at the same time. I want to be normal, but what if my normal turns out to be male? I don't know anything about dealing with the boys' gym room or their sports. From what Seb has revealed, bullying isn't as subtle as with girls, and I don't know if I want to have to physically fight back.

I run my finger across the *Gender and Sexuality* line in the table of contents and wish that I can just become a normal girl when this is all over. There is a spell called "Wish," but it is considered dark magic; I've seen it mentioned a few times in my uncle's papers and notebooks when I've discovered them unguarded. I doubt we'll learn it in any regulated school. My mind starts going down the path of possibility over that spell, but I quickly brush it aside. The rules protect us; I have to trust and follow them.

The professor speaks up after the tutor finishes reading the table of contents. "I know that not every change will be as intense for all students. Each of you is unique, and by the end of this course that will be even more true than it is right now. This is our first term where each of you will live at least part-time out in the mortal world, so we'll be taking our time with each category of transmogrification so you and the magic have plenty of time to uncover your innate self. You had a question, Haydar Plank?"

"Yes, Professor," the called-upon student said as he stood up, running a nervous hand through his wavy reddish-brown hair, so common in many mage families. I blink at him. He lives right across our street, yet I barely know him, other than the fact that he was on all the science teams at my previous mortal school. I've barely seen him here at Reinholdt. He pushes up his glasses before continuing, drawing attention to the freckles that cover his surprisingly pale skin. "What if the magic makes a mistake and we aren't happy at the end of the semester?"

I turn eagerly back to the professor, who is gently smiling while Tutor Lubit is frowning. "I have never known someone who was unhappy with their personal revelation. I don't recall any studies of the results that have cited such a thing either." She looks to the tutor, who has opened his class binder and is mumbling some words over a page.

At her nod, the tutor goes on to summarize what he'd found. "In the five-hundred twenty-seven years of this course, taught around the world under various names, there is only one case of reported misidentity. In that case it turned out that social and political changes in the mortal world were at fault, and the mage was simply allowed to live in the enchanted world."

"What does that mean exactly?" Haydar asks.

Tutor Lubit waits for the professor to nod, then paraphrases from the page. "Restrictive laws were passed in the host country a few years after the revelation, making it nearly impossible for the former student to live openly. I don't want to offend anyone, so I don't think it is important to name the country or the mage." He pauses and looks at the professor.

"Just give us the overview, please."

"Restrictive laws in the mortal world voided the mage's ownership of several businesses and even their place of residence. They were targeted by acts of violence against their property and self. After an emergency meeting, Central Council transferred all material goods into the magical realm and admitted the mage to full-time residency."

"Your concern is not unfounded," Professor Russo continued. "Mortals are particularly brutal in their drive to divide themselves into tribes. Since all your families have their primary residence in the mortal world, I would not be surprised if you have suffered bullying in your previous schools or neighborhoods. Yes?"

"Yes, Professor," we all reply in unison. I look around and see a few heads nod as well. I look down at my hands on my desk. *Can this be true? Have we all been bullied?* I look back up to find Haydar smiling and nodding as he takes a seat. He seems satisfied by the answers, but I have more questions about my classmates.

Maybe I should get to know Haydar Plank a bit more? I'll have to think about that. I wish I could see how Seb reacted to the question and answer, but I'd have to turn around, and that might draw unnecessary attention.

"Any other questions or concerns?" the professor asks. "Yes, Oswine Vlahović?"

I turn my head as the student stands up and asks, "How will people know we are us? I mean, the little things, sure, but what about the big changes?" *Big changes* is an interesting way to put it, coming from a boy who is easily the tallest in school.

Professor Russo and Tutor Lubit exchange a smile. "Good questions on our first day," says the professor. "It shows you all care. That's good, because sometimes this will be easy, and sometimes it will be difficult. To answer your question, the rituals and spells we'll use as the class goes along will leave a marker that other mages will automatically process. They'll know it is you, but they will also see the changes, as will you."

"What about mortals?" a familiarly loud and demanding feminine voice asks.

"Please raise a hand and be recognized," Tutor Lubit instructs with a frown.

"Sorry, Tutor, Professor. I'm Maxima Garriland." I smile when the girl stands up; she is always a bit too eager for the protocols in class, so I've seen her full-figured body standing up multiple times after she is called out by teachers. Wish I could be that bold for once, but it would draw unnecessary attention.

Maxima continues when the professor nods at her. "I live in Manhattan, so I run across mortals all the time. Will they recognize me?"

"With the eye and hair changes, probably, but not the full-body changes. Yes, that means you'll get firsthand experience of what others' lives are like if they have different ancestry or lifestyles," the professor tells us.

"After the final spell?" Maxima pushes.

The professor glances at the tutor, then nods a few times before answering. "The marker that allows mages to recognize you will allow us as your instructors, and each of you as co-casters, to recall your previous forms from throughout the course—such as those you currently have. Older and younger mages will not automatically remember your previous forms; the markers that have imprinted on them will change their memories. For any mortal friends or colleagues you might have, there is a spell you may cast to alter their memories when you first meet up with them in your new forms so they will recognize you."

All of us get very quiet at the idea of casting such a spell. It goes against the rules we've all had drilled into us repeatedly last year in *Mage Protocol in the Mortal World* class.

Before any of us can ask, the professor continues. "Because this is interfering with mortals' minds, it will be a decision you'll each need to make on your own. Some of us choose to simply start afresh with mortals; some of us simply don't interact enough with them to be concerned."

"Can it be done over the screen?" Maxima interjects. "I mean, I'll want to talk with folks on my phone or computer before I see them face to face."

"It cannot, so I suggest that those of you with mortal friends explain now that you will be quite busy during the term and you will need to cut back on such—social media, is that what they call it?" The professor looks to the tutor, who grins and nods.

"Well, crap," Maxima states, which starts a wave of laughter across the classroom.

"Indeed," Professor Russo agrees as she joins in. Once we have all calmed down, she asks, "Other questions? No? Let's continue with the introductory chapter. Tutor Lubit, if you will?"

"He isn't coming," I whisper to myself after glancing around the lunchroom for the fifth time since I claimed one of the smaller tables. Unlike the mortal schools I've attended, the room is not filled with long rectangular metal or plastic tables but solid wooden ones of various shapes and sizes. Seb has siblings, specifically an older sister, Victoria, whom I got to know a bit last year through drama club, so he wasn't shocked by as many things at Reinholdt as I was. I sigh now as I recall him telling me about the philosophy behind the round, square, and rectangular tables that could seat between two and twelve.

I take out my smartphone when it makes the sound I assigned to my grandmother—a K-Pop song without lyrics. She'd probably be offended if she knew, but she steers clear of most mortal matters unless they directly involve me or her patients.

Her text reads: *Are you remembering to get lunch?*

At one point I was skipping lunch and making myself throw up breakfast after I left the house. That was before I told my family about the bullying. When I started passing out at school in the mid-afternoons, they demanded to know what was going on. Since then, Gran has been very concerned that I eat enough and eat regularly.

I take a photo of my tray with salmon, potatoes, green beans, a whole grain roll, a light juice, and even candied orange peels. I'll probably eat half of it, but I'll taste everything. For now, the picture serves as a reply in a return text.

The text back says: *Good, good. Looks well balanced and now I know what not to serve for dinner. Lots of Love. Grandma.*

"Sorry I'm late."

Seb's voice makes me look up. He sets his tray down across from me but doesn't take a seat. He just stares, tilting his head to the side with a slight frown.

"Oh, oh, yes, it's okay, you can still join me," I reply. I'm still not used to the way girls are treated with more respect here at magic school. I know that our families tend to identify along maternal lines, but the politeness of most men and boys was really the biggest shock to me last year.

"I was talking to my teacher after math class," Seb explains as he pulls out the wooden chair and joins me.

"Did they put you in the wrong section?" I ask gently, knowing that Seb's lack of mathematical talent was an embarrassment for him back in the mortal schools.

"Nah. The teacher is also the assistant soccer coach," he states.

"Oh—oh, I see," I simply say, though I honestly don't understand how he can enjoy sport—*sports,* I correct my thought—so much. While I got bullied for what is between my legs, Seb was picked on for being on the smaller side of the boys when I met him two years ago. Not that I teased him; in fact, I offered him some words of wisdom after I witnessed him being pushed down my third day at the Brooklyn school.

"What are you smiling about?" Seb huffs, getting my attention.

"Nothing."

"Right?" he replies with a sigh.

I wait, but he just stares at me, his pupils going slightly dilated as he looks at me. "Fine. Since you won't eat until I tell you," I begin, but his frown makes me blurt out, "I'm remembering the first time we met."

Seb's cheeks turn red, and he picks up his utensils. "I don't want to talk about that, Blake," he states firmly as he starts to cut into his fish.

"I wasn't going to," I assure him.

We eat for a few minutes in silence, and then my uncle's designated ringtone—a series of typewriter sounds—makes us both start laughing out loud. "You better get that, Delmar is not a patient man," Seb tells me while pointing a fork full of speared green beans at me.

"I didn't know you were on a first-name basis with my uncle," I muse with a pointed look as I take out my mobile again.

"He and my dad are friends, so as long as I don't use his name to his face, I think I'm fine," Seb tells me before going silent.

My uncle's text reads: *Just checking in to make sure your first day is going well.*

I text back, not worrying about proper grammar as much as I do with my grandmother: *1st 3 classes good. Lunch w/Seb.*

My uncle's reply text: *Great. Say hi to my future ... nephew.*

I frown and feel my face heat up as I quickly reply: *As if! Go to sleep.*

My uncle's final text is: *As soon as I turn off this phone.*

"What was that that made you blush?" Seb asks as I put the phone back into my book satchel. I consider turning it off, but my family insists I leave the texting turned on while I'm in class just in case I need them.

"Delmar says to give you his love," I toss out.

"What the?" Seb sputters and has to set down his fork as he begins to cough.

Without thinking, I lay my hand on his and cast a small spell my grandmother taught me to help another control their breathing. I'm not very good at healing magic, but I can do basic assists like this.

Seb's entire body tenses up, but he stops coughing, so I pull my hand back. His eyes are going all moony, and he's blushing again. My uncle's tease rears up in my mind, but I just shake my head a few times and take a few pieces of dessert to distract me.

"We have history next," Seb offers after a few moments.

I nod, then add, "I hope this tutor has a better voice."

"I heard from Vickie; they're both great. Apparently, my mother went to school with the teacher and says she's a hoot and a half but takes history seriously."

"Good. I don't think I could handle another voice like this," I say, pronouncing the final few words in a monotone.

"I think we'll get into more of the rough stuff this year, like how mages were treated, so I can't see how anyone teaching those horrible events could not have emotions," Seb points out.

That's true. Last year was really a basic overview of our kind's history in the magical realms. Honestly, it should have been fascinating, but they made it so dull. This year we get into the past of the families who crossed over into or grew up in the mortal world. Periods of fear and hatred, even mass executions like the Burning Years in Europe, when entire villages were slaughtered for the sake of trying to find witches. My mother loved history, and I've looked through some of her old schoolbooks, so I have a general idea of what is coming, and I've shared that with Seb in the past.

But there are also things I haven't shared with him from those books, so I offer up insight. "I don't think every mortal society across the entire planet and over all of time has always hated us."

Seb shrugs and takes a bite out of one of the cookies he has on his tray. "I just hope it isn't boring, because you should be an ace at that stuff."

"You just say that 'cause you want to get me to tutor you again."

"Probably," he replies.

Our eyes meet for a second, and I can feel my own blush start as I see his cheeks redden. "So, tell me about soccer," I order as I get back to eating more veggies. I screw up my mouth as the sweet taste from the oranges makes a weird combo flavor for my first couple of bites.

Now we both relax more as he tells me all sorts of things about his job as one of the three student managers. By the time we've returned our trays and are walking toward our next shared class—history—things feel almost back to normal between us.

"Any changes yet?" Uncle Delmar asks me at dinner that evening.

I look up at him across the table and shake my head. "Just basic class information today. Tomorrow we start with eyes."

"Eyes first, huh? I always wondered why they couldn't correct vision problems during that class. I mean, shape and color are one thing, but it would be useful to actually improve something too." My uncle often shares with me his memories of the same classes that I'm taking. It can be useful on the weekends when he's around and I have homework, but he'll take off for work as soon as dinner is done tonight, so it feels like a stupid criticism, since we won't have time to really discuss it.

"What would healers such as myself do if suddenly all our physical challenges just disappeared?" my grandmother asks.

"People would still get sick, Mother. Babies would still be born. You'd have more time to help them rather than deal with petty things like glasses—which you don't even deal in," he points out.

"Physical challenges are character building," Grandmother amends. I think I feel her gaze slide toward me—my face burning with shame—but I keep my eyes firmly on my plate.

Silence reigns for a few moments, then Grandmother says, "I didn't mean you, Blake."

"You're perfect the way you are," my uncle adds.

I look up at him. I should really just be quiet, but I say softly, "Perfectly secret."

"It isn't anyone's business," Grandmother says as softly.

"That sounds a bit negative," my uncle replies as he sets down his fork.

"Sixth grade was quite traumatic for Blake, or are you forgetting?" Grandmother counters.

I feel my stomach tighten up at their tones of voice. They don't often fight in front of me, but when they do it always seems to be about me, my parents, or my uncle's job. It feels like it's about me most often.

"Blake, have you had any bullying since we moved to the States?" Uncle demands.

He means being intersex, having different-looking parts down there, but my mind goes back to the class's reaction to Professor Russo's question about bullying. I think of Maxima and how she spoke up, about how Haydar and Oswine voiced questions. I feel my heart beat faster as I make a decision and meet my uncle's gaze.

"Not about my body down there, no, but when we go out …" I look toward my grandmother. "… there have been looks, a few whispers, some comments."

"That's just Americans being less cosmopolitan," my uncle tosses out.

"Maybe, but Blake notices. I notice, too," Grandmother states. "Does that happen at school?"

"Reinholdt? Nah, I don't really stand out much there, not as much as some do," I offer.

"But before Reinholdt?" Grandmother insists.

I nod, and Grandmother goes into one of her lectures about how they have a duty to protect me, while my uncle insists that I need to learn to protect myself.

The discussion ends abruptly when Grandmother announces, "Blake has decided to keep it a secret. I know because of what potions she borrows, and which spells she's looked at in my books." My grandmother always uses feminine gender pronouns for me, while my uncle tends to vary them by what I'm wearing or my attitude.

I feel my mouth fall open at her statement. "You know—knew?"

"As if anyone can touch my things without my knowing," Grandmother simply says as she places her strong hands on the table and gives us each a lengthy stare.

My uncle and I turn to stare at each other before he smiles and starts to tell a joke. "I heard this last night at work. It'll lighten things up."

"No vulgarities at the dinner table," Grandmother counters.

"It isn't vulgar, Mother. It involves cats; how vulgar can cats be?"

I tune out their lighter conversation as the topic of my oddity is again pushed aside by mutual desire. All the while my mind is racing with mixed emotions.

At the end of dinner, I help float the dishes out to the kitchen where the adults will clean and put them away. I pause by the open space between the dining room and kitchen. Uncle looks over at me and asks, "Did you want to talk more, Blake?" His tone makes me believe that he doesn't really have time but would make it if I needed it.

Grandmother looks back at me too, her dark-brown eyes wrinkled up in worry.

"No, no, just not much to do in terms of homework tonight, so I was wondering if Gran has anything I could do?" I lie and hope it sounds close enough to the truth.

"You want to pay some bills for me?" Uncle teases.

I chuckle despite myself.

"No?" he goes on when I don't answer. "Did you have accounting yet in school?"

"Two years ago, but that's just mortal stuff," I remind him.

"Honestly not that much different, and half our bills are for mortals," Uncle says with a shrug.

"You can help me with some bottling for clients," Grandmother offers.

I nod, backing out of the open space. As I walk a few steps away, I hear something about telling someone about me, but I just press my lips together and go to my room to wait for the call to come help.

In my room, I take out my school journal and start another entry.

Dear Journal,

Am I too afraid of what others will think about me if they see my parts?

Why are they fighting about whether I should keep this a secret or not? Won't True You make that choice for me? Will Gran be disappointed if I'm not a girl at the end? Will Uncle be upset if I change?

Will I?

I wish I had someone to talk to about this. Not really, I wish it would all just go away. Maybe I do want to talk about it. Can't.

I stop writing and let go of my held breath. I focus on my breathing as Mother used to help me do. I can almost feel her arms around me, but today that memory seems too faint for much comfort.

"You're our special child," Father used to say to me every night before they put me to bed.

"I don't want to be special," I whisper and then write it in big letters in my journal. I write "normal girl" next and then again before Grandmother's voice interrupts me, relayed via charm in the shape of a small goat's head on the wall by my door.

"Blake! Come help me. I'm in the dining room."

"Coming," I send back by looking at the charm and speaking directly to it.

I put my journal back into my school bag and seal it closed with a touch on the symbols along the buckle. I head back to the dining room, looking around for any sign of my uncle as I walk.

"He's off," Gran calls out as I make my way to her. "Grab your apron and gloves; some of these medicines may stain clothes."

I do as instruct, and soon we're filling bottles and little boxes with potions, creams, and powders. We chat about each client as we pack up their orders. Grandmother never raises the issues of bullying, secrets, or my body—and I certainly don't either—so the evening passes quickly and enjoyably.

Chapter 2: The Eyes are Not Windows

The next morning, Seb gives me a quick wave as I walk into our classroom. He's talking with another boy from the football—no, *soccer*—team, and returns to their conversation right after. "So unfair," I hear him complain.

I slide into my seat in *True You 101* and take out my ritual kit and pen. I'm not sure which I'll need—probably both. Last night after helping Grandmother, I discovered that the textbook is full of graphs, charts, and text about the changes we'll be triggering. At the end of each chapter are questions we'll have to answer as we live with each change. No spells. Of course there are no spells, but I was hoping there might be so I could try a few things out ahead of time. Not that I would have broken the rules, but if they were in the book, I told myself that would just be getting a head start on the class.

The girl next to me rolls her eyes and makes a gesture back toward Seb's continuing complaint. "Seriously, does he act like that all the time?"

I blink, surprised that she's asked me a question, since I don't think she spoke more than a dozen words to me last year. I can't even remember her name, though I probably should learn it, since we're seatmates. There's something in her tone that annoys me, so I quickly reply, "I didn't ride in with him."

"Oh, I thought he was your boyfriend," she says softly, leaning toward me a bit. She has an odd scent on her brown skin, and I feel her light-green hair slip against my cheek when she gets close.

I feel my face flush hot, so I make myself laugh—a bit too loudly—as the rest of the voices in the classroom seem to disappear. I shake my head at her, but she just shrugs. I note that her oddly pale eyes turn back to Seb, and she smiles just a bit.

I open to the first chapter and turn to face the front of the classroom, trying to ignore the teenage drama unfolding around me. Dating Seb would be like dating my brother. We've known each other since we moved here. Plus it would be dangerous; it could reveal what I am, and I can't risk losing my best friend for something as stupid as dating. I glance at Nameless Girl and see that she's doing that weird flirting thing with her eyes— looking up and down in Seb's direction, fluttering her surprisingly long, greenish eyelashes. Of course, Burim—Mr. Handsome—is also seated in that direction, so maybe I'm mistaken. I turn my body and glance up to find him smiling back at my seatmate. And if Burim weren't enough, now Seb is glaring at Nameless Girl too!

I'm rescued from this stupid train of thought when Tutor Lubit comes into the classroom first and instructs us to place our journals into the box as we enter from now on. "It will speed things up in the future and keep latecomers from interrupting us quite so much." His tone of voice makes it clear that he doesn't think much of being kind to such students.

We file up row by row as the professor enters as well. She gives us each a smile as she passes by. She places a hand briefly on the tutor's shoulder, saying loud enough for us all to hear, "Thank you for taking care of this."

"Lunch today?" Seb asks me as I start to walk back to my seat. I nod and smile. He hasn't forgotten. Take that, Nameless Girl. Your flirting had best be for Burim, because Seb is lunching with me. I pause at the unwanted thoughts, and a student from behind bumps into me. *We are just friends*; I tell myself as I move to my seat. *Just friends*, I repeat as I take a deep breath.

"Everyone take your seat now," Professor Russo commands in a firm yet friendly tone. She waits until we're all seated, then tells us to open our textbooks to where mine is already.

"There is a mortal expression that the eyes are the windows to the soul. While that isn't quite correct, they can reveal our feelings and give hints of a creature's nature. Vampires, for example, have a thin ring of red around their pupils, while fae have a silvery twinkle in their left pupil."

As the professor pauses, our books show live-action examples of both creatures, along with a few others. Animated books are one of the things about mage education that has been a delightful experience since we all started at Reinholdt. Our history textbooks easily replace the video clips and films I used to see in mortal schools, though ours tend to be more honest, and thus more graphic. Or maybe that's just a reflection of being a sophomore now.

"Mages do not have such obvious and tell-tale signs in our eyes unless our heritage includes other creatures. However, the shape of our eyes can also reveal a creature's identity or ethnicity, just as it can among mortals. Take a moment and look at your seatmate's eyes to note how they are different. Then turn around and do the same with those sitting in front of and behind you. Go ahead. You can ask each other about your ethnicity or heritage, too. We need to be willing to share all this as we go forward."

Nameless Girl and I do as we're told. "I'm gonna guess either pure or mixed mage and mortal heritage—but multiracial," she tells me with a grin.

"Yes, to the second. Don't know about the first," I reply, leaving out my frustrations about how little of my family's history I know. That I *didn't* know wasn't obvious to me until last year when I overheard other students talking about family lines.

"Now you guess me," my seatmate demands. The pale color could simply be from a northern European lineage or some other supernatural creature, but it's the subtle bend of her eyes that makes me pause. "Your ancestors must need to let more light into their eyes, because they're so pale," I try to reason out. She grins and nods silently, urging me to continue. "The shape, though—is that non-mage and mortal?"

She nods and uses a finger to move quickly through the list of creatures until we see an image of a mermaid rise up out of a wave. The book zooms in to show us nearly perfectly round eyes, pale aquamarine in color. "I'm told that like five generations back on my father's side there was a maritime encounter," my seatmate giggles.

"And your hair?" I ask with a nod.

"Stay focused on the eyes," Professor Russo's voice makes us both sit back in shock. A glance around confirms that several other pairs of students have reacted the same way, so my seatmate and I laugh softly. After a few seconds, I introduce myself. "I'm Blake Trudeau."

"Hi, I'm sure we've been introduced before, but I think you hang out with the arts folks, while I'm in sports," she replies. "I'm Brizo Pachis; I'm on the varsity swim team. Natch."

I nod and think back to her flirting. Maybe all the jocks just tease each other or flirt without it meaning anything. "Nice to meet you again, then," I say offering my hand.

She takes it and blinks a few times. "You have nice firm hands, long fingers. Have you thought of sports? I mean, with your height you could do any of them."

I pull back without trying to make it seem like I'm freaking out as much as I really am. Luckily, I'm saved when the professor tells us to look at other eyes. The two students in front of us are both like me, mixed mortal and mage heritage but no other species. One of the two students behind us claims they have fae in their family, but the twinkle is really just an odd, lighter spot in their left eye.

After several minutes, the tutor gets our attention, and the professor continues. "Did you notice that even among pure mages or mortal mix mages, there were a wide range of colors and shapes? Tell me what you noticed."

After students offer their observations, the tutor directs us to turn to the next section of the chapter, and the teacher introduces us to the next concept. "However, our eyes, like mortal eyes, can demonstrate emotional or physical signs that we need to know about."

Behind me I hear Seb groan, and I have to stifle my giggle. He is more anxious to get on with the magics than I am, and I don't fully understand why it's so important to him when there is nothing wrong with him.

I ask him later when we're seated at the end of the drama and speech table in the lunchroom.

"Unless you're going to be a magister, who cares what other creature's eyes look like?" he counters. Since today we're at a large table that could seat twelve people, we're both speaking in whispers for the sake of faux privacy. I think most everyone at our table is our class or a year older, but I can't be sure. It's a big no-no to reveal *True You 101* to younger students.

"So, you'd be okay if a vampire asked you out on a date, then?" Only certain non-mage and non-mortal creatures are acceptable as mates. Our families have taught us that, both explicitly and implicitly. Mage culture shows us that in stories, in music, and even with what my uncle does as a news censor. Our *True You* textbook covers all possible combinations, but sometimes with citations of legal code or cautionary folktales about pairings that have gone wrong. Anything that must kill another fully conscious creature to survive is taboo. It does happen—my seatmate's family story reveals that—but that wasn't a marriage, nor was the mage involved going to become a mother, so there is a bit of a double standard at times. Not that I would point that out to Brizo. I need her to treat me like a normal girl and not do anything to renew her interest in my weird body.

"No, of course not," Seb hisses back. One of the other students at the table glances our way. Seb lowers his voice further. "I just want to get on with becoming who I'm meant to be."

I pause, then try to make my reply seem generic. "You know, we aren't just what we look like. We're more than body parts."

Seb's eyes go wide for a moment, then he shakes his head. "I know that, Blake. I just … for boys it's important to be strong, to be big, to look …"

"Handsome?" I ask. Seb blushes and chuckles, glancing around discreetly. I follow his lingering gaze off to one side to see Burim with the other sport jocks, but before I can say anything Seb changes the subject.

"I wish we had more classes together this year," he says a bit louder.

Before I can remind him about history class, the girl next to me glances over at us. "I have American literature with you, don't I?" she asks him.

"Yeah, I'm Seb," he replies with a nod.

"And I have math with Blake," the girl continues.

"Yup. This is Casey O'Hannigain. She's a junior and one of our best actors," I add to my introduction. Casey reminds me of my grandmother with her golden skin and straight hair, but Casey's is brown. Her wide, green eyes are unusual, and as I smile at her I wonder if she had those before she finished *True You* or got them after the final spell. Unfortunately, it's rude to ask such questions, and even though I sort of knew her last year, I can't recall her looking any different. That is probably the work of the final spell that our teacher told us about.

"Hey, I'm Victoria's brother," Seb says, adding the drama club connection.

"I know, she talks about you all the time," Casey says with a smile.

Seb gives me a horrified look, but I just shake my head reassuringly as Casey offers to help him with lit. "I don't get why we have to study these mortal subjects," Seb states and draws attention from the entire table.

"Don't you all live out in their world?" a boy sitting with us points out. I think he's a junior, but I don't know his name.

"Yeah, but my family's business is in real estate. I don't think my mother ever asks her staff or clients to discuss a great author," Seb counters.

"Maybe not, but some of us may want to go to a mortal college, depending on our talent reveals," Casey sighs. She's referring to the major class all juniors take. Much like with *True You*, they aren't supposed to talk about it with lower-level schoolmates.

The possibility of not having ample talent to have a career in magic is frightening enough that another boy at our table changes the subject by asking Seb about soccer. I'm saved from that dull topic by another text message from Grandmother: *Will I be shocked by your eyes when you get home?*

I smile in spite of myself and text back: *Spells start tomorrow.*

The next day, both my uncle and grandmother are waiting by the door when I get home from Reinholdt. My uncle narrows his eyes and leans in to get a better look until Gran shoos him back with a few pats on his shoulder. "Green but still creased? I thought the shape changed, too," he comments.

"Next week, the prof says," I sigh. "Apparently it would be too shocking for us to have both shape and color changing."

My uncle shakes his head, stands up straighter, and steps back. "I may be misremembering what my class was like, but I seem to recall that we made the changes faster."

My grandmother nods and moves back as well. "Green is a good color. Very natural, yet mysterious. I am biased," she adds, waving to her own eyes with one hand like a model we see on mortal television. "Of course, hazel eyes can appear green, too," she adds with a nod at my uncle. His eyes are that same kaleidoscope of pigments like mine, but a touch more green where mine are normally gold.

"Then we'd look even more alike, and who wouldn't want to be as handsome as me?" Uncle jokes, making jazz hands as he takes a step back then bows. My father used to be silly like that, I think. I can feel my smile fade as images of him playing with me rush through my mind.

"Or not," Uncle says slowly as he stops fluttering his hands.

"How about we let Blake do her homework while I finish up my final mixtures and you make dinner?" Grandmother suggests in her firm voice that means we will be doing as she says.

"You're making dinner?" I ask my uncle as I rebalance my bookbag on my shoulder.

"I am tonight—I may be late coming back in the morning. Big news stories on the horizon that might require my attention," he adds with a shrug.

I don't press him for more information because I know it won't make a difference. I head to my room to tackle my math problems first, figuring I can get through them before I'm called to the dining room.

"Blake," my uncle's voice urges me turn around before I'm too far away. My grandmother is nowhere in sight. He comes close and says, "You're a good kid, a great student. Your parents would be proud. I know they would be."

We just look at each other until I have to turn away or start crying. "Thanks," I whisper then bolt to my room and shut my door.

I put my hand on the intercom and command them to not bother me until I'm called for dinner. Not that my uncle would follow me in here to talk more, but I need to know I'll have some peace to just focus on numbers and equations.

I open my book, but my heart is pounding, and it takes me several moments to calm down enough that the symbols aren't blurred by tears. Then, I get down to the business of my trigonometry homework.

"Let me see your eyes," Seb demands two days later while we're eating lunch together.

I roll my eyes, then make them as wide as possible so he can see the pale gray color as I lean forward against the table.

He studies my face for a few moments, then just shakes his head. "I think they were better with green yesterday."

I frown and make a show of studying his own eyes. "Brown is not your color," I reply with a huff.

"Touché," Seb replies. He glances toward the soccer team, seated together along two tables about halfway across the dining room. He's directing his gaze toward Burim again.

"Would you rather eat with your sports buddies?" I ask, smiling when he blushes and stares at his spiral purple potato fries.

"Maybe tomorrow," he whispers before picking up a long curl and popping it into his mouth.

I copy him, exaggerating his movements until the other people at our round table are laughing at us both.

To retaliate, Seb starts using his napkin more like I do, but dabbing after every bite. I think we're both enjoying ourselves as the rest of the table copies us by mimicking each other's eating quirks too. Casey even goes so far as to make up a new way of eating, addressing her sandwich in a fake accent before taking a bite.

"Are you all having fun?" one of the professors asks when he stops by our table.

We all quiet down and go back to eating normally until he's moved on and several tables away. Then we all laugh again but don't start back up with the mimicking.

I can't help noticing that whenever he isn't talking, Seb's eyes keep going to the jock table. When we're finished, he doesn't wait up to walk with me to history class. He's talking with another student when I come into the classroom, so I ignore him and take my seat.

A few nights later, after dinner, I slink off to my bedroom and shut the door a bit too hard, causing the goat head to manifest and say, "Hey, take it easy."

"You're just a door, you have it easy," I reply, but of course it says nothing back. Unless I'm giving it a command, it doesn't really listen to me. I register that the very fact it's commenting seems strange, but I'm too worked up right now to do more than toss my journal onto my desk and take a seat with a huff of frustration.

Dear Journal,

I made a mistake teasing Seb last week at lunch. Today he wouldn't even wait for me to go into the dining hall. I saw him surrounded by the jocks. He only nodded in my direction when I waved. I am more than welcome at the drama table, so I ate there.

When I stupidly talked about it at dinner tonight, my uncle said that maybe it means Seb likes me and is embarrassed by the fact. That got my grandmother talking about the problems that being raised in only the mortal realm can cause between men and women. Except I'm not.

Nope, not going down that road again. I pull over the side mirror on my desk and stare at my face for a few minutes before writing more in my journal.

I think I like my original eye color and shape. The more rounded eyes were interesting, but this half shell design with the flatter bottom is a bit too unbalanced for my tastes, even if that's not uncommon for some mortals. which I'm not.

I'm looking forward to tomorrow because we start trying unnatural eye colors and shapes. Mortals have contacts that do similar things, so we can just be weirdos in cosplay for a few days. I wonder if cat-eye-shaped pupils would look cool?

I wish someone would have a meltdown in class when we do our daily check-ins, so we have to stop and linger longer on this unit. Maybe we'd run out of time and never get to gender and sexuality. Then I could just go on ignoring it and act like I'm okay.

That's a lie. I wish we'd just get to the end so I can finally be who I'm meant to be. Isn't that what Seb complained about?

what is his problem? Why is he ignoring me? I really ... he was making fun of how I eat, too. And he was copying others and laughing just as hard. Goddess, boys are so stupid. I hope I don't become one.

I close my journal when my door manifests its little goat head at the center, opening its eyes and announcing, "It's your graaaaandmother," in its bleating voice.

"Come in," I call out.

She enters and takes a seat on the end of my bed. I turn in my chair to face her. She studies me for a moment, her own green eyes taking in my current bright blue ones. "So, what will tomorrow's color be, then? Gray? Back to hazel, perhaps?"

"We're doing shapes now, too," I say, waving to my own eyes as she did hers last week.

"I can see. That's, meh, not so good, is it?"

I chuckle at her bluntness. "I'm not impressed by this shape either."

"And the color? Do you know what the next color or shape will be?"

"Not sure. It seems random," I reply.

Grandmother smiles. "I remember it feeling that way too, but I think it's the process of learning what you are. Feeling your reactions to the changes."

"Professor Russo has said that, too. Something about the spell not knowing until we know what feels most like ourselves." I pause and press my lips together before revealing, "What if we've known what we should be for a long time? Why can't we just become that and skip all the experimenting?"

My grandmother sits up a bit straighter and frowns slightly. "I'm sure the course is designed by experts. We've been doing this for centuries, Blake. It'll be all right."

"I'll become the girl I'm supposed to be?" I'm leaning toward her, pleading silently for reassurance, but Grandmother just sucks in a breath and looks sad for a moment before changing the subject back to eyes.

"When will you get to do exotic colors and shapes?"

I sit back and follow her lead in topic. "Tomorrow. Professor will show us how to tap into the illusionary plane to get other colors and patterns. Not for the entire weekend, though, just a couple of days unless the magics decide we need to freak out the mundanes for a while. Will that be random as well?"

Grandmother chuckles lightly at my words, then looks thoughtful before replying, "Again, I'm not sure it is as random as it feels, but as far as I know, we don't have any sirens, fae, or what have you in our family."

"Then why have those changes at all? It feels like a waste of time." Oh great, now I sound like Seb again.

"Empathy," Gran says, and I look directly at her. "Not only will some of your classmates with extra heritage have such traits revealed at the end of this year, but depending on your talents, you may need to have relationships with other creatures."

"Relationships?" I'm shocked by what I just heard, but Grandmother quickly explains.

"Did you know that some of my clients are part were, or an eighth vampire, or are even not mages themselves?" I shake my head silently, and she goes on,

"Of course you don't, because I respect them, not merely because they are my clients but because I walked in their shoes, as the saying goes. Even if it was only for a day, I learned what it was like to have to hide part of myself."

I want to point out that I already know what that's like, but my grandmother just continues to talk. "All of us feel awkward during this class—during life. I can still feel out of place at times, but because of where I am in that moment, not who I am."

It feels like Grandmother is offering a rare moment of intimacy, so I move over to the bed to sit closer to her. In an attempt not to lose this opportunity—learning more of my Gran's true self—I keep the focus on the class and our physical form. "When did you know what you were going to look like?"

"I don't think I knew until I saw myself during that last week of class. Of course, we didn't have as many mirrors and certainly no cameras like you all have around you all the time." Grandmother took her mage classes back in the early nineteenth century, while my uncle, like my mother and father, I guess, took his early in the past century. We all age like mortals until we're about twenty-five years old, then the process slows way down. My parents didn't have me until they were in their late 90s, maybe early 100s.

My thinking about these things must make me frown because Grandmother asks, "Are you worried about what will change, Blake?"

I'm terrified, but I shake my head. "I'm hopeful," I tell her, but I don't say that I want the true me to be a normal girl. I don't have to because I know she wants the same thing. A granddaughter. I won't be a substitute for my mother, but I'll be able to carry on the family line, since I'm her only grandchild by a daughter. While a male could technically pass on the physical traits, the magic wouldn't be as strong, and the family name would disappear.

She reaches out and pokes one of my tight curls behind my ear. "It will all be as it should be. We love you no matter what."

I want to believe that, but instead I use the opening to push for more parental information, even though I know this is probably a mistake. Maybe if I word it casually enough, she'll let something slip. "Did Mum turn out to be like you expected?"

Grandmother looks sad for a moment, then conjures a few family photos into her hands. The color tone of the photos is less bright and sharp. My mother is wearing drop-waist dresses or sparkly flapper style ones, depending on where she must have been for the photo. While the photos aren't the quality that I'm used to seeing, it is clear that she loved her long necklaces, big jewels (real or fake?), and Art Deco patterns. Last year, Reinholdt put on a play set in the Roaring Twenties, so I know a bit about the fashion.

"The changes aren't usually radical," she points out as she shows me the school pictures of my mother. The skirt of her school uniform is almost down to her ankles and white—meaning it was taken inside the magical grounds—unlike the dull colors our uniforms transform into when we go into the mortal realm. In the one from her junior year, her eyes are more almond shaped, lighter colored but not green, and her bobbed hair is a touch lighter as well—curlier than the photo from the previous year. Her skin was still a darker version of Gran's, reflecting her paternal heritage.

"And Uncle Delmar?"

Grandmother makes the photos disappear and starts to stand up when I capture her hands with my own. We stare at each other for a moment, and when she begins her excuse, I finish it for her. "Your uncle lost his ..."

"... in a tragic fire. Right."

I release her hands, but she raises one to caress my cheek. "I'll start looking. Maybe some can be found at his old school. It may take time," she cautions me.

"Really? You'll really look for them?" I ask, and she just nods, so I jump up and hug her tightly. "Thank you, Grandma. It would be so reassuring."

She tilts her head to one side and arches an eyebrow in curiosity, so I quickly add, "I mean, he's always telling stories about his life. I sometimes think he's exaggerating, so I'd like to be able to check the facts, as my new history professor says."

Grandmother nods with a smile, accepting my explanation. "I can also ask your father's father. They may have some too. Anything to make you feel better," she tells me. My paternal grandmother died a few years ago, but we still keep in touch with Grandpa, even though he lives in the magical realm most of the time.

"If you don't mind," I add, though my tone is more demanding than pleading to my ears, "I'd love to see more photos of both Daddy and Mommy."

"I know where I put the photos of your mother. Emma was a beauty, so I have a lot of them; I just put them away, in a safe space," Gran begins. Her voice turns a bit melancholy, and I almost wish I hadn't asked, but I do have a right to know more about my parents. I know I do.

"If you need me to move anything or carry anything … I am strong, Grandma," I remind her. That makes me pause. If I become only a girl, will I stop being as strong as I am now? No—no, women can be strong; they can have muscles. I've seen female bodybuilders.

Grandmother stops my rush of thoughts by pulling me into a hug and whispering, "Thank you."

I let her go, but I have this suspicion she'll forget about my uncle's photos entirely.

Dear Journal,

As predicted, Grandmother found more photos of my mother, but not of Uncle Delmar. She also had a few of my dad from when he first met Mom and a lot from when they were dating. Only a couple of photos from before True You for Dad until we can hear back from Grandpa. I'm not holding my breath for that to happen.

I've laid what I have side by side, and I can see parts of me from both of them. If I let my vision blur, I can see Uncle Delmar too, between them.

I concentrated on those photos for a long time, hoping my talent might manifest and give me some magical revelation, but no such luck. It would be cool to see the truth behind lies, right? I know that means I think they are lying to me.

I think they have been for a long time.

Anyway, this is supposed to be about classes, so classes are mostly boring. Seems no one wants to teach us more magic this term while we're all changing. I could take the other courses in the mortal world. As the older kids told Seb and me earlier, some of us may need to have careers in the mortal world, so we have to know all this stuff.

Eckhart

At least I got my cat-shaped pupils like I was hoping. Slightly larger than my own, rounder in the middle, but with longer edges and a bright green around the vertical slit. Really made the bus driver give me a second glance. He asked if they were a test for Halloween, and I just smiled.

Seb got vampire eyes ringed in red, and dark as the deepest night, in the center of the odd oval shape. He's decided that he has to wear sunglasses until tomorrow morning. Serves him right for always hanging out with his jock friends and ignoring me.

Chapter 3: Tangled Variety

"Now that is interesting," Victoria Hiles explains when I walk into the theater meeting. Today is our first day of hair colors, types, and lengths. Victoria is not just a junior and the student director but also Seb's older sister, which makes her the source of much of his anxiety since we came to the Institute last year. We've known each other since my family moved from London, but it's only with my joining the drama and newspaper clubs that we've started to become friends. She's the only other person in the room so far. I smile and do a little twirl, using a hand to feather out my straight, blonde, pageboy-style hair. "Feels weird," I comment as my fingers slide right through the strands.

"No doubt," Victoria replies, giving her long blonde hair a toss while she chuckles. She looks back down at the script she was reading when I came into the auditorium.

At least she didn't comment negatively on the change. Given how slowly we seemed to get through the eyes section of *True You*, I thought hair would be a mild change—maybe it would give me looser curls or even something like my grandmother's smooth mane, even though hers is turning gray. I feel my heart slow down as I hope that Victoria's reaction reflects what the rest of the drama club says or doesn't say.

I sit in the same row with one seat between us and take out my notebook for theater. I glance at Victoria. She's tall and thin, shaped like a model, except for her ample chest. I find myself hoping once more that when I become fully female, I'll look half as good as she does. Those thoughts are rude, so I try to do something useful to get my mind off that envy. I thumb through my theater notebook to waste time and seem like I'm not her stalker, but in a few moments, Victoria's voice catches me by surprise. I feel my face heat up as I lamely ask, "Would you repeat that? I was looking over things."

"What do you want to ask me about my stupid brother?" I look up and see that she's turned to face me.

"How do you know I have a question about him?"

"I could claim that I'm reading your emotions, perhaps your thoughts, but not only is that forbidden, it wouldn't make much sense, given my question," she retorts. "I've noticed he's stopped eating lunch with you and sitting next to you on the ride home. I've seen your wistful face. Plus, you're blushing right now."

I frown and glance away from her. There are rumors that Victoria's talents do lie in the mental realm, but right now I find how correct she is to be annoying. In my mind, she's always looked and acted like this, so why am I surprised at her blunt question?

"I've been your age not that long ago; I can recognize when friends start to feel differently about each other," Victoria continues.

My uncle's teasing comments about Seb come rushing back to me. Do I like my best friend like a … a boyfriend? No, no, no, I can't have feelings like that until I'm sorted out. My face must be showing my inner turmoil because I flinch when I feel a touch on my hand, which is tightly gripping my notebook.

Victoria's long fingers are gently against mine, but they pull back when I jerk. She fixes me with her light-green gaze. "Come on, Blake. I won't tell Sebastianus anything you say. I'll even cross my heart on that."

For mortals such a pledge is exaggeration, but for us, with the right ritual, it would be binding. I knew that even before my first term at Reinholdt, because my family made sure to stop me from saying such a thing, even though I saw it on mortal telly and read it in their books over and over again. I'm sixteen; I'm sure what I'm worried about is objectively no big deal, but still I hesitate. She hasn't done the ritual; she could still tell Seb. I can't risk him or anyone else learning about me. She keeps looking at me until I sigh, straighten my posture, and meet her eyes again.

"Did something bad happen to him on summer vacation? He's been acting all weird since he got back," I explain, putting a sincere edge to my voice that isn't a lie. I have been wondering about that since they returned to our neighborhood.

"Guess I'm too close to have noticed," Victoria muses softly. "Look, Blake, just like you, he's going through some changes right now, and not just the *True You* ones. When I was your age, I saw a lot of friendships fade or change, but I also made new ones. I still care about my buddies from childhood days, but it isn't the same. It can't be the same; that's not how life works."

"I know," I say with another sigh. I do know it from all those embarrassing books and pamphlets Grandmother's given me over the past two years. Mostly that information focused on girls, so I only got half the information I wanted. Correction: I only got maybe a third of the information I wanted. I've peeked at some of the boy's materials at the mortal clinic where she works part-time, but it wasn't as helpful as I'd hoped. There was nothing about someone like me in any of those pamphlets. I can't really be sure that what I've found online is real or if my body actually works like a mortal's does. Currently all access to mage knowledge is restricted at school to the current or past classes we've had. Sexual organs and sexual orientation won't come up until the spring.

I don't have time to expand on my question to Victoria because other club members, including the supervising professor, Salomea Hermans, are showing up. I blush when Victoria reaches over and gives my nearest hand a squeeze.

"Everyone, take a seat," the professor says. "I'm going to hand out the list and the reading assignments. I've approved all of these with the school board." She hands out the binders, which contain descriptions of a dozen potential plays. She floats up to sit on a tall stool at the front of the room so that her short stature is compensated for. The Hermanses are known for their cross-species experiments, and after her sophomore year, the fairy—or perhaps gnome—ancestry affected her height when she finished *True You*. Everything is the correct proportion, just much smaller. While crossing over to the mortal world would be particularly challenging for someone like her, the theater professor has done so several times and has a good dozen acting credits listed on the mortal Internet. Drama is important in the magical realm too, because her bio for the Institute lists her as having a position on a couple of theatrical groups across the barrier between worlds.

"Any of them with naughty parts?" a newcomer asks as she takes a seat a couple of rows behind me.

"Depends on if you mean sexy or criminal," Victoria tosses back. She lifts the binder, already open to one of the plays.

"Both?" the newcomer replies, and several students laugh.

"The answer is yes then," the professor states, and more laugher erupts. Professor Hermans smiles back for a few moments before her face gets serious and we all follow her lead.

I smile at Nanuk Holst as he sits down next to me. This year I'm working under his guidance to learn about makeup and costuming, including magical and practical special effects. Nanuk is always dressed and styled in the latest fashions from both realms, combining them in breathtaking ways. His beard and mustache must take a chunk of time every morning, but the fact that he even has them as a junior is pretty impressive. I wonder if that was a thing that *True You* did for him.

Last year I did stage building, but it felt a bit too butch for my tastes. Still, I wave at the senior who is leading the team, because she was a fun person to work with. We're all in this together; we are all theater club, and any personal choices we make can't be allowed to damage our group cohesion. Oh, wow, did I just quote Professor Hermans?

"We have a third person this year in costuming and makeup, and I can see why," says Nanuk, drawing my attention. We quickly glance through the list of titles, and I can start to see why, too. We've got two ancient mortal dramas, a high wizard comedy, three musicals—one from our realm, and the others were probably on Broadway or West End—a high wizard historical piece, and a science fiction thing I've never heard of before. In a few minutes, that newbie sits down in the row in front of us with apologies. "Just don't be late for our meetings, or you are out!" Nanuk warns her in a low but firm hiss.

"I like that better," Uncle says bluntly when I step into the living room where he's watching something on the mage screen. The conjured screen appears to cover the entire wall behind it—including the shelves, the items on them, and the huge mortal telly he bought the first week we moved here. I frown when I notice the show is the news, because I know the few seconds I have before he closes the screen down is all I'll be allowed to watch. My grandmother and uncle pass-spelled the screen so I can't even watch whatever it is teens watch in the magical realm.

The screen dissipates, leaving behind the black view of the widescreen telly and the shelves crowded with a mixture of mortal and magical decorative items, books, and magazines. My uncle stands and gives me a good look up and down. "You'd think it would have been this style yesterday," he muses.

"Is Blake home?" Grandmother's voice reaches us before she comes into view. She's coming from the direction of the dining room, still in her medical garb from the clinic, meaning she put in extra hours today. She clasps her hands over her mouth with a sound of delight, then moves toward me.

I stand still as she touches the long loose curls falling in mahogany waves over my shoulders and down my back. "The color is good, maybe a touch too much copper, but let me see your eyes." I look at her and make my eyes a bit wider. She pats my shoulder lightly as she says, "Oh, your normal hazel and shape."

"It's just hair these two weeks," I remind her.

"Seems like it should build on what you've done. Figure out the eyes, then just try combinations with the hair, and so on," Uncle comments.

"Is that how the course worked when you took it?" I ask him, inferring permission to inquire about his past since he opened the door on the conversation.

"Ha! No, it was as illogical as yours. I think I felt the same way then about my incremental changes," he vaguely offers.

Grandmother's mouth opens a bit, then she presses her lips together for a moment before saying, "I can't remember everything I thought when I had the same course, but I do know that I was always very anxious for the big change, and terrified at the idea of it."

"I imagine every student feels that way," Uncle states as he leans against the back of the chair. "That is lot of hair, though. Pretty," he quickly adds when Grandmother gives him a frown.

"Many ways to style such hair," Grandmother offers.

"I'll only have it until tomorrow's class, so I'll just pull it back if it gets in my way," I reply with a shrug.

I subtly step back and shift my school bag on my shoulder. "You worked a longer shift today, Grandma? Can I help with anything while you change or relax?"

"Ah, my good girl, Blake," she replies with a wide smile. She runs her hands down her uniform and replaces it with a bright-red, patterned shift that she calls a housecoat, though I've seen similar items called housedresses here in the States. "If you'd like to order pizza for us, I could focus on a big order that came in," she tells me.

My uncle's mouth opens in an exaggerated look of surprise at this offer, but that only makes her shoo him off with a few choice words. "I'll get the pizzeria menus," he states before leaving us alone for a few minutes.

"Grandma, what happened today at work?" I push just a bit.

She heaves a big sigh and then motions to the couch, so I sit down and face her as she takes a seat in her chair alongside it. All the furniture is arranged in a semi-circle so we could easily watch telly as a family, although we rarely do. Normally socialization and conversations happen around the dining room table, so whatever she's about to tell me must be big.

"There was a racist attack this morning on one of the subway lines," she simply begins. "Not the one you ride to Manhattan, another one. Some of the victims were registered at the clinic, so we took them in. It was more than we're used to dealing with. *We* couldn't save one." She puts an emphasis on the plural, suggesting that she could have used her magic, but doing so is frowned upon, though not completely forbidden.

I move over on the couch to be closer to her chair and ease my bag onto the floor next to me. "Oh, Grandma, that must be hard. I don't know how you make those decisions. I don't think I could."

She smiles and reaches out to capture my hands. "Maybe if you have the same talent, you can work somewhere you can do more. For now, your caring helps a lot."

Grandmother stands up, so I rise as well just as my uncle reenters the living room. "Get a vegetarian one for me, but enjoy yourselves," she instructs us before nodding and walking toward the hallway that leads to the bedrooms.

My uncle frowns at Grandmother's back, then turns to me with an overly wide smile. "Veggie for her—yuck. Do you want your own, or you want to split one?"

A quick memory flashes through my mind of our home in London. My father is saying the same thing about Grandmother's pizza request while my mother is looking down at me and telling me that the pie we'll split will have extra cheese for me but not the spicy meat.

In the present, I look at my hand, which my uncle is holding. I glance up at his worried face. He's moved closer to me, his free hand grasping the menus, but also nearly touching my arm.

"Blake, are you okay? You got pale for a moment, and skin tones are after eyes and hair, right?" he asks with a chuckle, but his tone is serious.

"I was just remembering the last time Mum and Dad got us pizza before …"

"Oh!" He pulls back like I've burnt him, then reaches out to pat my shoulder with another forced smile. *How many of his smiles aren't real? How many have I been overlooking?* Before I can ask, he speaks. "I hope that was a good memory, Blake. I know—your grandma aside—that your folks and I loved pizza and liked a lot of the same toppings. I'm probably less picky than the two of them, actually."

My uncle seems to be babbling, and it's unnerving, so I interrupt to assure him, "Yeah, a good memory, really good." He stops speaking and looks at me expectantly, so I take the menus from his hand. "We should see if there are any coupons or specials, but I'd like my own pizza, something with extra cheese, not a lot of spice."

"Fine, fine, I'll have peppers on mine, then, to make up for it," he jokes. I get out my smartphone and look up our favorite restaurants to check out any deals they are running. Within a few minutes, my uncle is ordering three pizzas, all mediums so we can have leftovers later.

As we wait for the delivery, Uncle Delmar just sets the menus on the table next to his chair and motions toward the couch. After I've sat back down, he tosses me the remote. "You're a great kid, Blake. I think Mum's gonna probably stay in her room to eat or be in the dining room, so why don't you pick a show for us to watch together?"

"Even a teenage mortal fantasy drama?" I tease him.

He predictably makes an exaggerated wince, then nods slowly. "Argh! If we must, we must. Just not witches."

"No, no, that's just ridiculous," I agree before finding this werewolf show I've been hearing about on our favorite streaming service. Who cares if they get werewolves wrong when the leading actors are so fine to look at? For the first time since the semester began, I almost feel relaxed at home as we binge three episodes.

"How do I even?" one of the other girls from *True You* is whispering harshly at her reflection when I come out of the bathroom stall and into the shared washing area.

It takes me a moment to remember her name, but I don't need to use it when I come over to her. "Let me wash up, then I can help," I tell her.

Day three for me is bright red hair that is so fine that I've been terrified of brushing it too much. It has long loose curls, similar to what I got yesterday, but the humidity is going to make it puff up like a balloon when I go back to the mortal realm. I can't say I'm a fan, but at least it's interesting to give it a chance.

Once I'm washed, I rummage through my backpack and take out my original styling products, which I still have on me. You can't plan for what the spells will do, so I haven't stopped bringing my haircare kit. "Don't try to comb it or brush it like you have. Use this to tease out the tangles, and then apply some of this to smooth it out," I tell her as I set each item on the ledge under the mirror.

"Isn't that caving to racism?" she asks, her bright-blue eyes looking a bit moist. Her skin is what my grandmother would call 'aged porcelain,' so between her eyes and her hair—which is even tighter and thicker than mine used to be—she makes quite an interesting picture.

I want to burst out laughing, but instead I just shake my head. "It's just making it less of a pain to deal with. Trust me on this."

She watches me work on a small section of her hair, then tries it herself. In a while, we've managed to gather it into a few groups and tie those up with ponytail holders I have in my backpack. "Cool," she comments when we're done. "I'm Eva Reijinder—we sometimes ride the same route to get to and from Brooklyn," she says, holding out her hand.

"I'm Blake Trudeau," I reply, shaking hands. "I've seen you on transit, but you generally get off the bus line before me."

"I think we have Mortal Bio and Writing classes together."

I ponder this for a moment and then nod. "Yeah, but you sit at the front of the row or with your buddies."

"Rah, rah, let's go team!" she fake cheers, making us both giggle and earning a few looks from other students going in and out of the toilets. "Oh, gross! Wash your hands, dude!" Eva calls out after one boy, who just flips us off as he continues walking. One of the weirdest things about magical school has been the unisex bathroom facilities.

"Why do they do that? I mean they use their hands—or at least one, don't they?—to, you know, help aim," she speculates, making a crude gesture that makes us both burst out laughing.

I could tell her what I do, but I don't know if that's what a normal boy does, and I'm an only child, so I can't claim to know what a brother might do. I do know from my research that everyone like me is different in terms of what our body parts look like or how they function. I definitely can't tell her all of that, so I just shrug as our giggles die down.

"In here your hair is looking nice, but I can help with what's going to happen as soon as you step outside," Eva suddenly tells me.

That's right. She's a redhead with curly hair nearly reaching her waistline. I smile and nod. In a few minutes we've exchanged haircare tools from our backpacks with the promise to switch tomorrow in class unless we get the same or similar hair.

"If we don't have the right tools, there's a strip mall not far from where I get off the bus that has, like, nothing but hair salons and supply shops. If you'd be cool with getting off the bus there, we could get what we need together," Eva suggests with a sincere smile.

I pause for a breath or two. My mind quickly runs through what Victoria told me earlier this week about friends. Haircare may be superficial, yet it is necessary. "I'd love to do that."

"Awesome! Good luck with your hair," she says as she shoulders her bag. "I have study hall soon, but if I don't use it, I hardly get anything done at home."

"Good luck with yours too," I reply before she's walking off toward the designated study room.

I turn back and adjust my hair again, checking the barrettes along the points, and spritzing it with more moisturizing hair spray. "Just stay neatly, smoothly coiled," I tell the locks. I shake my head and pull on my own bag so I can get to my next class. Maybe I'll grow to appreciate it more as the day goes on.

Dear Journal,

Contrary to popular belief, not all jocks and cheerleaders are jerks. Eva Reijinder and I talked today because she got hair sort of like mine in today's change. I got hair like Eva's.

Helping Eva reminded me of Mum, but it wasn't sad like I was expecting. I didn't even really compare them until I was on the bus back home later looking at Eva sitting up front with another one of the cheerleaders. I used to help Mum style hers, and she taught me how to do mine, even though I had curls from my father's North African heritage, not the straight, silky strands my mum had from her family.

Seb hasn't said more than a few words to me each day for over a week now. He's being a tool. He can hang out with his jerky sports buddies if he wants.

But again, not all jocks and cheerleaders are jerks. Just Seb and his friends.

I'm not sure how I feel about hair this fine, but I think the color is kinda cool. Here's an image of me to remind myself of it.

I put my smartphone on the journal and say the short spell we learned last year that can copy information from a mortal device into the book. I use it for photos, but not often.

Really, if I ended up with short, red, fine hair, and I had almond-shaped blue eyes, would it be so bad? If the rest of my body becomes normal, I can handle all this minor external stuff. I know I can.

I'll even wash my hands every time I use the bathroom regardless whether or not I end up a boy.

I shudder at the memory of that guy walking out of the stalls and Eva telling him off. In a moment, I'm laughing at it all. I'm feeling almost light and relaxed again until I realize it, and I feel all my worries push forward again.

"That is not a natural color," my uncle says when I sit down at the dining room table at the end of the next week. Every evening he's been making a comment about my hair, normally positive, though he wasn't thrilled by the blondes or the shorter lengths.

"Yeah, I know." I touch the strands of the smooth, spiral locks as he continues staring at me.

My grandmother smiles slightly, but she says nothing. Uncle Delmar sits back in his chair and looks me up and down. He shakes his head. "Pink and blue stripes. Rather obvious, don't you think?" he mutters. My grandmother's eyes go wide.

"I didn't consciously decide on this," I retort, my voice low and trembling slightly. They both look at me in silence as I continue, increasing in volume with each sentence. "And what if I did pick this pattern? Do pink and blue have to be gendered? You know it used to be the opposite; Mum taught me that, and I remember from some history class or show on the telly, too. Just because you both are ashamed of me ..."

"We are not ashamed of you!" My mouth snaps shut at my uncle's interruption. "We, they, none of us are ashamed of you, Blake. There was just so much drama at the hospital when you were born, and then the bullying starting in year seven ... we don't want you to suffer that."

I narrow my eyes at my uncle. "How would you know about hospital drama?"

My uncle's eyes go wide as he opens and then then closes his mouth. Grandmother turns a glare upon him, and they share a look between them.

"Were you there, Uncle Delmar?"

My uncle looks from Grandmother to me and then back to Gran again. Finally, he sighs. "Your parents told me. Mum, I mean, your Grandmother told me. It wasn't just my job offer that brought us here, you know."

My stomach tightens at his words. Is he saying that we left the UK because my body isn't normal? I knew at some level that our move was related to me and those damned brats at school, but to hear it said out loud feels like a punch to my gut. I want to scream at them, but it isn't their fault; they didn't bring me into this world messed up. They aren't my parents; they can't be responsible.

No! I chide that blame and ball my hands into fists around the utensils I'm holding. This happens in the mortal world too. No one knows why, how, or when someone whose body doesn't match one sex or the other will be born.

What if how I was born was related to something my parents did or didn't do? The thoughts I try to control flood back. I've been thinking about what might have caused me to happen for years. I've been asking my uncle and grandmother but getting no answers. My stomach starts churning now, the feel of being punched turning to nausea. I set my fork down and stare at my food. The words I want to say, the questions I want to repeat, just kill my appetite.

"Blake, I didn't mean anything bad," my uncle begins.

This time I interrupt. "May I be excused? I have homework to finish."

"Of course, dear, you go do that, and I'll bring you in some soothing tea and a biscuit later," Grandmother says. Out of the corner of my eye I see her place a warning hand on my uncle's arm.

In about half an hour, I hear my uncle leave to go to his job. The rest of the house becomes quiet. If I listen, I can hear Grandmother moving about, probably in her lab next to the kitchen. I can hear the buzz of insects outside my window. I can hear my heart beating faster as I start to think about the past.

My mother and father went out one evening when I was only six and never came back. It wasn't unusual for them to suddenly go out, either at night or during the day. They had cover jobs in the mortal world. My mum was a paramedic in London but did something for the magical realm that they never talked about. My father had the same magical job, I'm sure, but he was an assistant writer of some type for the Labor Party for many years. Their going out a couple times a month wasn't unusual, but they always came back—until that night.

My uncle Delmar arrived the next week, hugged my grandmother and me, then moved in. They never really talk about the "accident," as they called it, just as they never say more than "your body" or "your condition" to me. They never use the proper terms for what I am. Intersex. I had to find that term on my own, and I'm still not sure if that's the right word in the magic realm or only in the mortal world.

I force myself to do a bit of homework—maths and mortal bio—then go online. I return to the intersex facts website I found years ago. Less than two percent of all babies are born with ambiguous sex organs in the mortal world. In the enchanted world? I still can't find that information, because I only have access to pages approved by Reinholdt, and those are locked according to your year at the Institute and the classes you have taken or are taking. I have to wait for our first sex switch to see if I'm as rare among other mages as I am in the mundane world. Not that it will matter, because this class will sort me out, I remind myself.

I click to see the latest news article on the main site. Someone's been killed—again—and the defendant's excuse is fear at learning about his colleague's condition. Most of the comments under the article express sorrow and empathy, but there are also declarations of hatred. I glance at the counter on the right-hand side of the page that keeps a tally of violence, both self-inflicted and by others. Intersex and trans people, even though we aren't the same thing by a long shot, are killed at an average of one a week around the mortal world; numerous more are attacked every day. The suicide rate is one of the highest as well. This is all assuming such violence is being accurately reported.

I close down my browser and take a deep breath. I keep looking at the monitor, torn between the need to know I'm not alone and the terror I'll feel if I check back on that counter. With a firm shake of my head, I stand up and decide to go to the dining room to finish my homework.

I set out my textbooks, journal, and school-issued tablet. Nothing from the mortal world now to distract me except what is churning inside my mind and stomach. I take out the history book and open it to the assigned section questions.

"Oh, Blake, I was just going to bring you some tea and chocolate biscuits," Grandmother says when she comes into the room several minutes later, wiping her hands on the apron around her waist. She could do all the housework via magic, but she's told me numerous times that she finds it relaxing to be hands-on. I'm sure she knows that I use domestic arts when I'm helping ever since that class last term, but unlike my uncle, Grandma doesn't expect me to do everything her way. She at least understands what I want and tries to help me be a normal girl as much as possible.

Right now, she makes a gesture and whispers a word, and the tray with two cups of tea and a plate of cookies floats into the room. Making treats is one thing, but apparently carrying a tray qualifies as work, not relaxation. She sits across from me and takes one cup and a single cookie. Sometimes, if I'm careful, I can get my grandmother to reveal snippets of truth as she did a couple weeks ago with all the photos of my mother. I never did get photos of my father or uncle, but I put that annoyance aside for the moment.

We eat quietly until I ask the same question, I've asked hundreds of times. "Why does Uncle Delmar think he can tell me how to live my life? You don't even do that, and I've known you a lot longer."

Grandmother frowns, chews her bite, and swallows it before she sighs. "He made your parents a promise to raise you as his own, you know that."

"You've told me that; I don't know it," I counter. Grandmother's eyes widen for a moment, but she stays silent. I sigh and rub my hands over my face a few times. "I'm not a little kid anymore. You and I could get along just fine without him. The house is paid off—your medicines, ointments, and teas cover most of our bills—and the clinic still pays you, even if it isn't great. I could even get a part-time job at school or elsewhere. We can support ourselves."

"Is this all because he raised his voice at you at dinner? He loves you, dear; he just wants what's best for all of us. He's been through some things before he joined us, things that make him worry for us—for you—more than we did before the accident. Not that we could have foreseen everything ..." Her voice trails off.

I stay silent for a few moments, trying to figure out what she's said, but the tone of her voice is what keeps the mixture of pronouns from making sense to me. I didn't mean to make Gran feel guilty or to stir up those memories. I can almost visualize the two agents—from whatever job my parents were involved in—at the door telling my grandmother that she needed to come with them. I can hear the sharp cry she made before she covered her mouth. I can feel her hands on my arms helping me into my coat and then handing me over to a nice lady who gave me a soft toy unicorn and told me that I was going to take a little vacation with her. I never even got to see their bodies to say goodbye to them. All these memories almost distract me from my true speculation.

I take two breaths, then a third, before I voice a new, dangerous statement. "He doesn't look like Mum; he doesn't look like you." By mortal standards my mother would have been part Asian and part European, my father part African and part European. I look at Grandmother and see no African features at all. I bite my lip as she stares at me. "Is Uncle Delmar really just my uncle? He looks so much like me, far more than Mum or Dad do in their photos."

I'm not foolish; I know that my current class could result in my becoming something different from what I am. I can't remember my older school friends as anything else, but the photos of my mother indicate that some records will remain. The textbook says the final result won't be a total change, even if the results are extreme in one area. Genes and heritage are always a factor.

"Is Uncle Delmar's father a different man than Mum's?" That wouldn't be unusual even in the mortal world, but among mages, who trace family lines along the mother's side, it seems reasonable to assume that the answer could be that simple. I want it to be that simple.

Grandmother's face reddens a bit, and then she shakes her head. "As I'm sure you are learning from *True You* this term, ancestry isn't everything, but it is important. The Fates know what we truly are and what we need to become, so we can be the best mages and protect each other. Sometimes that revelation comes years after school; sometimes it makes perfect sense immediately."

She stops talking, so I turn her words around in my mind for a few moments. Is she saying that Mum and Uncle have the same father? If that's the case, then that means the Fates are a factor I really hadn't considered and which the textbook does not lay out. I look up at Gran and feel my mouth fall partly open before I stand up and start babbling. "You mean like, the final spell knew that my parents were going to die, so it made Uncle Delmar look a lot like me?"

Grandmother flinches at my words, and probably my tone of voice. She shakes her head as I continue.

"That means that they knew they were in danger, but they still took those jobs—that assignment, whatever it was—because no one will tell me anything. They still had me knowing that I'd be an orphan!"

"You aren't an orphan!" Grandmother yells.

She puts one hand over her mouth, then frowns when I glare back at her, letting my anger spill out further. "My parents are dead. I'm not dumb, I've figured out that they aren't coming back, even if they are off on a 'special mission,' as you sometimes claim when you aren't saying they had an accident." I make angry air quotes with my fingers before taking a deep breath. "You could just tell me the truth, and then I wouldn't keep constructing these fantasies."

Grandmother is trembling now, and I feel a wave of shame rise in my stomach. But my anger at my uncle's stupid comments forces that back down as I spit out my final words. "By the time this is done you'll have the grandson or granddaughter you've always wanted. Then maybe you can tell me the truth about what happened to my parents."

I push myself away from the table, grab my books, and stomp back to my room. I pause, then put the only ward I know on the locked door. It won't keep either Grandmother or Uncle out, but at least it makes me feel like I have some say in my own life.

I glance at my computer and ward it too, so I can't casually start searching for more horror stories about people like me. I step in front of the full-length mirror and stare at my hair. Why couldn't it have come out just pink or blue? Why does my body have to be so mixed up about the core issue of what I am? I know what I should be. I know what I want, what I need. Right? "Just decide!" I yell at my reflection.

Fates. My uncle, my parents, my grandmother. Did they all know this would happen? Did *True You* give them hints that they just ignored? Uncle can't be that much older or younger than Mum. I don't even know if he is younger or older because we never celebrate his birthday.

I put my hands over my stomach as it rolls with my feelings. Why don't we celebrate his birthday? Why don't I know if he's Mum's younger or older sibling? They can't be twins, right? The final spell wouldn't make twins look so different, would it? Could it?

I take a step toward the mirror and look more closely at my face. He looks so much like me that he could be my twin, my brother, not my uncle. I turn my face toward my door and notice ripples of energy coming from it, meaning that my grandmother is probably trying to send a message through or open it up. I repeat the ward, then look back at myself.

It can't be the Fates; the book would surely tell us about that possible twist to our true selves. It's our textbook for the most important class we'll ever take. It wouldn't leave out something that important.

I turn and take out the photos, then take out the few I have of my father and my uncle. I align the most recent images of my parents on the top of my bed. I pick up my uncle's photo from last year when I caught him off guard and took it. I swallow and lay it underneath their photos. I take a photo from me that was taken at the start of the school year and place it next to Uncle's.

"Are you my brother? But how?" I ask out loud as I stare at us.

I know my parents were older by mortal standards when they had me, but not so much for mages. That doesn't mean that they couldn't have had a child before me—but he's decades older than me, and that's just not possible. Right?

"Now you're just dizzy," I tell myself out loud as I gather up the photos and return them to my desk drawer where I've been keeping them.

I sit on the edge of my bed, frozen by all the impossible things racing through my head. There is magic that manipulates time. We learned at least the names and definitions of the types of magic last year, even though we won't get into any of the how-to until next year. What was that called again?

I flip through my journal to access my school notes from last year. I take the correct ones from the pocket dimensions that the book houses and quickly scan through them. Chronomancy, the manipulation of time with a list of specialties. Nothing about aging someone either younger or older. That just means it isn't legal magic, or at least not until you go to university.

"That might make sense," I say as I return the notes to the journal. "If they had a child but knew that they might die, they could have aged him up to protect me. It would explain why he seems to have little idea about my classes and his answers aren't very good or consistent about his own past," I reason softly.

I stand up as my mind starts going into overdrive. "Or what if Mum was pregnant when they died, but the doctors rescued the baby? Then the Central Council felt guilty about it, so they took him and did these spells? That would be so mean to do to a baby!"

The energy coming off the door draws my attention again. Normally, Grandmother wouldn't push so hard, but then again, we usually do what she wants after only a look or her tone of voice. I repeat the ward, forcing all my willpower on it, and the attempts to break through dissipate.

I take a deep breath and reconsider everything that has been going around in my head. No, no, my parents wouldn't use magic like that. Gran would never accept a grown-up version of a grandchild and miss out on raising him. Would she?

She doesn't tell me the truth, not the truth that matters. She ignored the facts about my parents never coming back. Can I recall a time when she hasn't hidden something from me? She's always lived with us; that, too, is common among mage families and not unique in the mortal world. Yet my earliest memories of Gran are less formed than the ones of my parents. Maybe she wasn't as involved with raising me as I thought. Maybe what I perceive as her support is really manipulation. Why?

My stomach churns again, and I have to run to my en-suite bathroom. I make it to the toilet just in time to empty out dinner, tea, and cookies. I heave a few more times, then wipe my mouth off as I start to chuckle.

I am going crazy, my thoughts all dizzy and out of control. To think that I would be important enough for all that conspiracy when I'm not even a normal girl must be insane. I feel like the bathroom is spinning as I squeeze my eyes tightly shut. Weird. I feel a cold rush of air across my face, but when I open my eyes, I'm just in my bathroom.

Which stinks! I take out my cleaning supplies and get to work dealing with the mess I've made. This lets me push all those stupid thoughts back deep down inside.

Chapter 4: More than Skin Deep

"Now do a turn for us," Victoria tells me when I enter the theater room. I look around at the other club members there. I love these people because they include all years, genders, races, and ethnicities; their one commonality is a love of theater.

Monday morning Professor Russo explained that during the next few weeks the changes will be more than just skin color, even though most of us who grew up in the mortal realm might think color is the defining feature of race or ethnicity. Hair, eyes, and—even to some extent—the shapes of our bodies will change to reflect someone of our age and sex who has the ancestry the spell will mimic for us. "You won't have to worry about any diseases or food intolerances that might also be connected to ancestry. We're just building on what we've done already in the term," she explained.

I stuffed down my worries about being a non-normal sex and tried to relax during the ritual. I was actually pleased by the results, so now I pivot, showing off. My hair got longer, thicker, and straight as could be. My skin lightened and then took on a reddish undertone. My features changed a bit, but frankly they stayed more generic than I thought they would.

Wigheard Flowers, our lead actor for two years, stands up and circles me a few times. Every move he makes flows smoothly, and each piece of clothing and makeup he wears highlights his features perfectly. Out in the mortal world, he'd be signaling that he's gay, but I've never asked, because…well, it isn't my business, and I'm not interested in him in that way. "I'm thinking Native American or First Nations," he finally declares as he stops to one side of me and turns to face the rest of the group.

"That's what I thought too," I agree.

"Did everyone end up looking like this?" Efemena Dixon, our special-effects chief, asks as she stands and gives me a lopsided frown. She's the best technomage currently in the school, combining magics and mortal equipment to create effects and lighting for the three shows we put on every year. She's my age, but she skipped a couple grades, so technically she's a senior.

"Rude, since you know the answer," Victoria chuckles. "They let the spells randomize so everyone still has to learn to get along, particularly if they cross back to New York."

I nod. "Professor Russo said it would be something we were completely unfamiliar with each time," I explain.

"Yeah, it was a rough three weeks," Victoria shares. "The mortals just couldn't figure out why so many different kids kept going into my house. My mother told me that a neighbor came to make sure we still lived there." We all laugh a bit, but now I'm feeling nervous. The neighborhood I live in is diverse, but on public transit you can meet all sorts of loonies.

"So glad I don't have to deal with that," Efemena states with a shudder.

"You can't live only in the enchanted world," Wigheard counters. He puts a hand on my shoulder and leans in to whisper in my ear, "I like it; don't listen to her," before he goes back to the script he was looking over when I entered the room.

"Since my mother's family came home during the Burning Years, none of us have left it. There's really no need to," Efemena retorts with a toss of her vibrant red curls, whose deep tones against bronze skin would make Eva look even more fragile by comparison. I smile as I think about the cheerleader I'm starting to think of as a friend.

"And yet you use their technology so very well." Professor Hermans' words make us all turn toward the door as she walks in—all one meter of her poised and commanding. "Let's all be honest, somewhere in our families are mere mortals, even in mine," she continues as she floats up to stand on a stool. Efemena just sits down and rolls her eyes, but we all ignore it. "Let's talk about this production. We have the rest of the term to comment on Blake's various forms," the professor instructs us.

I take my seat next to Nanuk and get out my notes from the makeup and costuming meeting we had earlier in the day. We settled on a space opera, and that is going to require a lot of work for our department. As the professor begins checking in with each team leader, I take a few moments more to look around at the club members and feel comfortable.

I let my bag fall to the floor of my room when I enter two days later. I don't even pause when Uncle and Grandmother greet me. I lick my lips, which don't feel right to me yet, even though today's change happened hours ago.

What the hell is wrong with me? I can't even say the words out loud, because I'm ashamed of how I felt the moment I realized the nature of the change.

Race is complicated, yet simple. Both in London and here in New York, people perceive me based on my skin color, my hair style, and my clothes. I've had folks whisper things I bet they didn't think I heard, not only when I've been out with Uncle or Grandmother, but when I've been out by myself.

The slurs I heard so loud on the ride home today … I can't even think them. Except I did, when I first looked in the mirror that appears in front of each of us after we cast the class spell for the day in *True You*. My dad, my uncle—they'd hate me for the things I thought.

Each day in class, Professor Russo has reminded us to be gentle with ourselves and each other. All of us have absorbed the mortal ideals; they are part of us, and our reactions are our reactions. We control what we do, not how we initially think or feel. For the first two days, I don't think I had a problem with what looked back at me in the mirror. Monday I was gorgeous, if a bit androgynous. Tuesday, I looked like an Arabian princess, or really femme prince.

I force my feet to move until I'm standing in front of my full-length mirror. I can feel my breathing speed up. I just can't raise my head to look.

I know that my father's family is a combination of different mortal racial groups going back at least three generations, just as my mum's is mixed for at least four. I might now look like my great-great-grandmother on Dad's side, or I might look like a generic black girl I could see anywhere on the telly, outside on the streets, or in the shops.

I tell myself I'm not racist, because how can someone like me be racist when I'm so many different peoples at once? The fact I've been telling myself this for years probably means I am racist, I realize, and I snort in frustration.

"I'm not!" I state out loud and look up at the mirror at the same time.

I dig deep and pull out positive words, saying them aloud as I look over my reflection. "I have a smooth, clear, ebony color that works well—no, that goes *perfectly*—with my hair and eyes. I can see my emotions right in my big eyes," I add with a swallow as I notice them glisten. "My lips, nose, and eyes are … well-spaced. They all go together." My voice strains for a moment, so I bite my fuller lower lip and then nod firmly before continuing.

"I'm very symmetrical, like a model," I declare. I feel some tension drain from me as I see that is completely true. I don't think my face was this well laid out before. There is a tiny darker spot just there, but that would be a beauty mark, right? "Right!" I state with a smile that grows wider the more I look and tell myself every positive thing I can find, repeating them over and over until my room's intercom announces dinner.

I look at the little goat and answer back, "I'm coming!" I pause and then decide to change my clothes.

I look at myself in my mirror again, forcing my eyes up at the top of my head, which I haven't praised. So short. I've always had longer hair; it helps with the feminine image I try to project. My mum and gran always had longer hair. I swallow and bring up one hand, then the other, to rub over the couple of inches of tight hair. I helped Eva; I helped a few others who had hair this coarse—even one this short not long ago—so why am I on the verge of crying again?

I suck up my tears and blink several times. I can do this; I have to do this. I consider my dress, then nod a few times with an idea. I go to my hair accessory boxes and pull out the older ones. I touch one black, silk case with a green butterfly on it, opening it up to see the collection of pins, combs, and barrettes inside. These were my mum's. Grandmother gave them to me on my thirteenth birthday, but I've never worn them since that day.

The little goat opens its mouth, and my uncle's voice asks if I'm okay.

"Just a few more minutes, please," I say back.

I take a breath, then start trying different adornments from the box.

Both my grandmother and uncle's mouths fall open a bit when I walk into our dining room wearing one of my nicer dresses, a pair of heels, and the array of sparkling green butterflies in my short hair.

They don't say anything for several moments, and I start to look away, planning to claim I feel sick, when my uncle declares, "Now I feel underdressed." He says a few soft words and makes a gesture. Now he's in a suit with a tie that matches the color of my dress—a metallic green that brings out the fact that my eyes are dark brown instead of black right now. After a moment, I can see a silver thread in the tie that outlines a few butterflies.

"I feel like I undercooked," Grandmother giggles, drawing our attention. She's now in a white cheongsam with matching green flowers and small fluttering butterflies around them. "I'm so happy to see you wear those again, Blake," Gran replies, which makes all three of us start to cry softly.

"We could get the formal dishes, or just …" my uncle suggests, making a few impotent hand waves to draw our attention back to the now.

Grandmother rolls her eyes before casting the spells that turn our table from an everyday setting into the most elegant looking feast I've seen. "It will still taste like the food it is," she warns us.

"Good, good—magical calories are the worst," Uncle teases. He holds up a hand as I start to move my chair. "Let me get those for you, ladies," he offers.

At my grandmother's nod, he goes to her chair and pulls it out for her to sit, then eases it back closer to the table. He repeats the same for me, patting my shoulder as he does so. We exchange a look, and I can see in his face that he knows what I'm feeling and why I've done this.

"We'll have our own fancy holiday," Grandmother declares when Uncle is seated as well.

"Then we must have atmosphere," he replies before conjuring up some music and lowering the lights.

"May I?" I ask, using a domestic spell to change the lighting into various colors which add to the festive feeling.

As we eat the food that doesn't taste as it looks or smells, we chat about weird holiday ideas that pop into our heads. By the end of the evening we've created an event called *Sacred Emerald Unicorn Feast* that must happen at least once every decade. Collectively we've done what we've always done, ignored the things that make any of us uncomfortable, even if it's blatant.

When Grandmother rushes a small cake out in honor of our new holiday and lets us decorate it, I let the realization that I'm no better than them in admitting to and dealing with my feelings fade off to nothing. Right now, I feel like no matter what I look like at the end of the school year, my family will love me as a young woman.

"Some of you are not journaling," Tutor Lubit scolds us at the end of the week. "It's important to share your experiences."

"But we start off each class with these group check-ins," a boy's voice grumbles from somewhere in the back.

"Which I monitor, and which have been nothing but awkward chatter that has nothing to do with what you're currently experiencing," the tutor begins but stops when the professor raises a hand.

"I've been—we've been—where you are. Frankly, by comparison to what we see on the mortals' TV and in their publications, particularly online, it's much worse out there for anyone perceived as a minority," Professor Russo states. This just makes me, and I'm sure my classmates, more self-conscious. As far as I know, neither of our teachers live in the mortal realm and probably haven't for decades. Yet each of us has spent most of our lives in it. How can Russo and Lubit understand anything?

"As Tutor Lubit said, we circulate around the room when you chat with your neighbors, and we read the few words some of you are writing," she continues as she moves, catching the eyes of students as she goes. I turn my head to follow her toward the back of the class. "They don't align," she finishes, and the boy she is looking at blushes and sinks down in his seat.

I turn back to the front of the classroom as the professor returns to her podium. "From now on, anyone not journaling properly will be asked to my office, or Tutor Lubit's, to give us an oral report on your experiences. Is that clear?"

"Yes, Professor," we all answer in unison, but our voices sound hard and distant.

Professor Russo sighs but holds up one hand again when the tutor frowns and starts to step forward. "You're probably thinking: What the heck can these two magical realm dwellers understand about how my week went? You are correct that both of us currently live here in the magical world most of the time. I was born and raised in eastern Europe at a time when the mortal world looked like it was in its death throes."

I pay more attention now, because we've been looking at the world wars period in history recently. I might have used that information to try to learn more about my family. Even in Europe, what you looked like and where your ancestors were from played a big part in how you were treated. The States aren't the only racist places on Earth, after all. I was so focused on my own image in the mirror each day that I couldn't think of much else.

I blink when the tutor speaks up. "What you see here," he says, using one hand to motion down from his face along his body, "is much lighter than I was born. Where I was born … I know that outside in New York City, what you look like can draw all sort of horrible attention, but at least the government isn't rounding you up and jailing you, as they did when I was your age. I made a choice to stay in the magical realm after university because I knew no matter how many marches and elections there were, this," he taps his cheek a couple of times, "would keep my options limited in the world on the other side of that door."

"We aren't trying to be mean," the professor interrupted gently. She placed a hand on Tutor Lubit's arm, and they exchanged interesting looks of affection that didn't seem romantic. He nodded and stepped back to let her take the floor again. "We may seem old to you, but we went through these classes in the 1960s and 1970s. Much of what you experienced last week, we lived out, either for those few weeks or during the course of our entire lives. We know that talking about this, writing about this, is important. Not only for you right now, but to help the final spell work properly."

I glance over at Brizo, who meets my eyes. We both look down when the professor continues, because over the past week our conversations have been completely superficial, as charged.

"I'm going to ask you to please talk to each other honestly and to journal about what you can't bring yourself to talk about. Will you do that?"

This time the agreement comes in sincere replies scattered about the room. I look over at Eva, who gives me a firm nod before she speaks up. I look at Brizo and the students in front of us, but I don't open my mouth.

"Come on. Everyone, I need you to make this promise to yourselves and to each other, not just me, not just

Tutor Lubit. I need to hear you say you'll communicate better, both speaking and journaling."

"Yes, Professor," I say once, then I say it more loudly. Brizo slides her hand over the shared table and taps her fingers once as she repeats her pledge, too.

"Good, good." Both of our instructors look exhausted, I realize, as they lean toward each other over the textbook on the podium.

"Now let's start exploring the interracial and interethnic differences, as the mortals would say," our professor continues with a soft smile.

I smile too, because these sorts of combinations will be more what I'm used to than the previous week was. If I'm more like I was, maybe I can use the smaller changes I'm about to undergo to get more information about my family, tap into their experiences with *True You* by saying what the teachers shared with us. If I'm careful enough, I can get more pieces to solve the second biggest mystery of my life.

"Professor!" I look up to see that Maxima has another question, as she does almost every class meeting. It shouldn't annoy me, because she's brave enough to ask about the things I often find myself thinking.

"Yes! Question?"

"This week will be more mortal world combinations. When do we try out the exotic forms?"

Beside me Brizo huffs in annoyance.

"Let's be careful with our words. That goes for everyone. 'Exotic' can be an objectifying term," Professor Russo instructs. "We'll tackle the intermagical combinations next week. I think, as many of you learned last week, these mortal possibilities can be more of a challenge than you may believe. The majority of you may already define yourself as multiracial or multiethnic, but the combinations are numerous. There will be challenges, even though today the changes will be variations on your biological heritage."

I frown at this information. Logically, I know that. But how different can I really look? How many different ways can African, Asian, and European ancestry mix?

Of course, I get payback halfway through class—immediately after we cast the spell—as I look into the mirror that appears in front of me. I sigh as our desks move around to reorganize us into discussion groups of four. At least I'm always with Brizo, even though today we're joined by two others we haven't talked to since the mortal eyes week.

"I think the eyes are the biggest difference," Brizo begins, and I blink before realizing that she's pointing to her own. "I mean, strip out the mermaid, and all I have is European, right, so why this tilt?"

"I don't think Europe is as isolated as we believe," the only boy in our group states. "I mean, mortals were traveling and having sex—" he flinches when his desk mate slaps his arm. "Sex isn't a bad word. How do you think any of us came into this world?"

I'm amused by their familiar teasing but catch Tutor Lubit's eye as he pauses by our group. "I get what you're saying," I offer quickly. "My eyes are a lot rounder than I was expecting for how dark they still are. I felt kind of surprised—no, shocked."

"Yeah, yeah, shocked," Brizo repeats.

"I don't know anyone in my family with blue eyes," the girl who slapped her seatmate states as she motions up to her own dark blue ones. "Seriously, it's been brown, brown, brown, maybe a hazel here and there, but even with the eye week, I didn't get close to this."

"What?" Brizo exclaims.

I look around and see that Seb is just two groups over, appearing to be more invested in looking at Burim—who is sitting across from him—than talking.

I refocus on the three people in my group and get back into our conversation. As our group really shares, I feel myself tense and relax in cycles over the course of the next twenty minutes.

"Hey, Blake!" I turn at the sound of Seb's voice and find him jogging toward me. We're both heading to lunch, but I haven't really talked to him since that last time we ate together weeks ago. He stops and looks me up and down. "That's what I thought," he says after a moment.

"You thought what?"

"We're both the same interracial group, so maybe we can help each other out," he offers.

I blink slowly at him as I soak in his words and try to decipher his meaning. He's acting so casual, as if no time has passed since we were mimicking each other at a table just through this archway. I take a deep breath, stopping myself before I say something that might draw attention to us. "I see," I say and start walking away.

"Oh, come on!" He sprints a couple steps to catch up with me but lowers his voice as he continues talking. "I mean, aren't we still friends? Doesn't Professor Russo say we should help each other out with these changes? I stood up to that dick who tried to grab you at the bus stop three days ago!" he tosses out.

I halt and adjust the straps of my backpack. Just because he casually stopped by my side to glare at a clearly drunk or drugged-out jerk who sidled up next to me, he thinks that makes up for all his ignoring me for weeks? He didn't even say anything to me that day; he promptly moved back a few seats and followed until I peeled off to my driveway.

A few people are glancing at us now, and I feel my face heat up. I turn around and glare at him. "Fine, but you eat lunch with me, and you be nice to me until at least tomorrow's class," I dictate.

Seb blinks at me with his darker eyes, his darker skin turning a bit red in the cheeks. I don't wait, moving toward the lunch line. "I didn't know I wasn't being nice," he mumbles as he catches up with me.

"You've been a jerk," I hiss at him.

"I'll do better, okay?"

Even with his features changed so much, I find it difficult to see him as anything other than the best friend I've been mourning. I want to hug him, but instead I bump him with a shoulder. "Be less of a jerk. I'm not asking you to hang out with me all the time," I reassure him.

We walk toward the cafeteria's daily offerings side by side, but I still feel a distance between us. When we get to the line and put our trays on the rolling counter, Seb leans a bit closer than necessary to me. "Blake, sometimes I wish you were on the soccer team," he whispers.

His voice sounds sad—but something else too. I can feel his body close to mine for another moment, then he takes a step back. I'm too surprised to do more than nod or shake my head at the kitchen workers who ask which items I want.

By the time my tray is filled, I've calmed enough to lead us to the table where I've been sitting. Seb pauses next to me, so I turn and follow his gaze to his sister's face. Victoria snorts, then motions for us to sit, while the rest of the table moves over a bit to let us sit on the same side, with me between the two Hileses.

There are a few moments of silence, but no one at the table asks why Seb is here. How could they, when another club member has his boyfriend, who's a science nerd, sitting with us as well? The point of Drama Club is that we act it, we don't cause it, as Professor Hermans states at least every week during our afternoon meetings.

Victoria, our de facto student leader, finally breaks the tension. "I hope you're all ready for this full-table reading, because we have a lot to get done."

"That's a special Friday after-school meeting, right?" one of the newer club members asks, looking around the table with a panicked expression.

"This Friday," I gently state, earning a smile and nod from Victoria.

"All of your Fridays after school and your Saturday mornings are ours now," Wigheard states firmly. "I hope no one has forgotten that, because we actors will be putting in the effort, but we need all of you to make this work."

We all agree while Seb eats quietly. I catch him glancing at the jocks' table just once, frowning at Burim, who is sitting next to some cheerleader. Seb glances at me with a weak smile, so I give him a brighter one back, and his mouth widens.

The conversation switches to a few comments from our older magical realm residents who have seen our current play performed elsewhere. "We'll do a lot better," Efemena assures us as she discretely moves her fingers to manifest a few ghostly butterflies she has designed for the show.

"Yes, we will, because I know that Hermans has invited a critic she knows to check us out on the second night," Victoria reveals in a hushed tone.

Everyone at the table, except for Seb, sits up a bit straighter at the news. *At least it won't be opening night*, I think as I pick up my spoon to taste some of the pot pie I chose.

"What the heck combination is that?" my uncle asks with a chuckle when I step into the living room two days later. He's already dressed for his job in slacks, shirt, a pullover sweater vest, and comfortable shoes. His briefcase is sitting on the entry bench, and I slip off my backpack and let it make a thud as it settles next to it.

"You have the entire weekend to look like that; you'd think the spell would consider that" Uncle continues as he puts on black-rimmed glasses. He doesn't really need them yet but wears them when he heads into the nighttime news desk where he works.

"Thanks for the reassurance," I grind out, a bit louder than I planned. I wince as I rub my hands over my too-large face.

"Is that Blake?" Grandmother's voice makes me spread my fingers and look at her. She pauses and blinks a few times, taking in my larger form. Our uniforms adjust to the spell, which is good because of all the changes I've been through; this week has been rough, and today's change was the worst. Subtle body changes to reflect ethnic groups is one thing, but I think I put on at least a stone of weight—more than a dozen pounds.

"Lower those hands; let me get a look," Grandmother orders gently but firmly, so I do. She takes a few moments to look me over, directing me to turn around with a few hand gestures. "I like it."

My uncle snorts and earns a glare from Grandma. "You get your unhelpful self to work if you can't be supportive of your … family," she orders.

"I'm sorry, Blake," my uncle begins, only to be shooed out the door by Grandmother.

Once we're alone, she puts her hands on my arm and guides me to the dining room. "I have a wonderful dinner I've kept warm, since I doubt you ate much during rehearsal."

"How did you know?" I ask as I frown, remembering how much my tummy kept urging me to eat but how looking down at my body made me think twice and thrice. I didn't do anything other than drink an iced unsweetened tea the entire two hours.

"I've been kind of waiting for the body changes to become more intense," Grandmother tells me as she physically brings in a tray with a covered plate and a cold glass of lemonade—my usual drink on even the most wintry of days. "I remember them myself. They can be jarring to live with, though usually that's separate from these changes," she adds as she sets the tray in front of me.

I sigh at the starch-heavy meal she uncovers when she lifts the lid. "I really shouldn't," I start, but her tsking makes me stop.

"Whatever you look like right now, your metabolism is the same as it was, which means you need to eat. I saved dessert for us to share together, and I want that, so you eat up."

I take a few bites, and then find myself nearly inhaling the food because I'm so hungry. After a chuckle and head shake from my grandma, who has joined me at the table, I make myself slow down.

"How was the first stage rehearsal?" she asks me.

"It went okay. Mostly the actors and the special effects walked through the scripted stage directions. We went over Nanuk's notes for all of us and got some of the cutting and layouts started."

"I remember how well you did with the stage crafting last year. Are makeup and costumes similar?"

"Well, um, I guess, just more detailed," I offer. I'm really trying to enjoy this more feminine work, but I kept finding my eyes glancing over to the worktables where the stage crew were going through their plans. "It's gonna be a lot of work before the show because the costumes are very detailed. Then, during the play itself, there are a few costume changes we'll need to help the actors with."

We make small talk about the play for a while, then Grandmother takes a note from her pocket and slides it across the table. I recognize Professor Russo's family crest as well as Tutor Lubit's on the unbroken seal. "Is there a problem with *True You* that you want to talk to me about, Blake?"

"You didn't open it," I point out. The last few bites on my plate are unappealing to me. *What could I have done wrong in that class?* I've been journaling; I've been talking in groups. I don't talk much in the course itself, but heck, with folks like Maxima and Haydar around, who else needs to?

"I thought we'd open it together," Grandmother says, but she lets the note stay on the table between us for a few stressful moments until I push it back toward her. She picks it up and snaps the seal, allowing its magic to fully activate.

The note floats just a couple inches above the table and then opens, letting Professor Russo's voice emerge. "To Ms. Trudeau and Mr. Trudeau, the guardians of Blake Trudeau, my student in *True You* this year: Greetings! I want to encourage all our students' families to be extra supportive during this second half of the course. We are about to experience changes to our bodies that most of us would otherwise never have. I want you to know that Blake is doing well in this course."

My mind perks up at that comment. I listen to my teacher lay out what we've done, mentioning my work inside and outside of class related to the magics we are channeling. I pay close attention to the list of changes that are coming. My grandmother is nodding as she listens seriously, almost more focused on the words than my being at the table. My uncle will need to listen to it on his own now, and I really hope he does, because as reassured as I am by the tone and content, the future changes my professor runs through sound scarier than I thought they might be.

I retreat to my room after dessert, feeling a bit relieved as well as pleasantly full. I tackle all my other course homework for a couple hours then think about the note. We aren't to the part of the class that I desperately want to get through but knowing that I'm doing well is encouraging. If last Wednesday's and today's changes have taught me anything, it's that none of this is as superficial as skin color.

I take out my journal and turn to the correct section for the course. I stand up and look in my mirror, heave a sigh, and run through the positive notes I can make, as I did last week, until I feel as solid inside as I look outside.

Then I sit down at my desk to start writing.

Dear Journal,

I thought people looked at me before, but these past two weeks have been mind-blowing. Thank the Fates that we learned some defensive spells last year.

It's shocking how many different vulgarities there are based on skin tone and perceived ethnicity. I hope I don't end up just one category, because none of these tests were unproblematic.

I thought European might be the easiest, and in some ways it was. No one followed me around shops or kept an eye on me while I browsed. Women mostly ignored me or gave me catty glares, but at least they weren't constantly trying to touch my hair. The men and boys out in the mortal world catcalled me more, some of it downright rapey, or maybe I just noticed it more when the racist attacks stopped.

When I look at myself in the mirror it just seems so boring. I hope the real me isn't a Becky, because yuck!

In other weirdness, what the heck did Seb mean by saying he wishes I was in soccer? Does that mean he hopes I become a boy when this is over? I've been thinking about it, but I've never told him; I'm sure I've never even hinted.

Maybe being a boy wouldn't be too bad. At least it would be normal, right?

Chapter 5: Size Matters

"For the next two weeks, we will be experiencing weight changes," Professor Russo tells us in class. It's on the schedule and in the textbook, but what it means isn't really clear. The previous weekend we had a break from these changes and had some questionnaires to answer in our journals about body shape and size. Similar multiple choices preps have been part of the earlier chapters too, but this one felt more intrusive to me. The lights in the room dim, and Tutor Lubit brings up a display of our answers while the professor continues to talk.

"For two weeks, we looked at heritage changes that affected skin colors, subtle facial shape, and, for some of you, occasional minor weight changes. I want to say that even though it took repeated nudging, you were all able to write about and discuss the biases you had, which everyone has, mortal or mage."

The first question displayed is "Are fat people lazy?" and the answers create a murmur of comments until Maxima says loudly, "Screw you all!"

"I know that seeing these is going to hurt some of us," the teacher interjects before anyone can reply, "but please remember that you had to answer quickly, and you could not change your answers. Most biases are internalized and automatic. What we do with our biases should be a matter of choice. These next weeks are about helping you recognize those biases by experiencing life in a different body, and therefore helping you make better choices going forward."

The next question in front of the class is "Are skinny people sick?" and the answers are a bit more spread out. Any teenage girl could have predicted that, but I'm surprised to see so many people answered "Yes" or chose "Depends on the situation" versus just "No."

The professor calls on a boy from a back row whom I don't really associate much with. "What if our body already is one of the categories?" He looks rather tall and thin, a condition he'll probably grow out of as he gets older. I feel my mouth fall open a bit at my thought. Is that a bias?

"For those of you who might be considered under or overweight, your body will adjust up or down to help you experience the average build for that week. If that is you, please try to help your classmates adjust to their new bodies with the understanding and patience you wish people gave you," Professor Russo replies, looking at each of us in turn as she emphasizes that last part.

Am I thinner than average? I think I'm rather androgynous looking—not much difference between my waist and hips, not much of a bustline, barely enough to justify wearing a bra. If I became average … that would be awesome!

"Why a full week?" Eva is now asking, so I pay a bit more attention.

"I know that we've only had to live with most of our changes for a day or two. Ideally, I'd make you each experience the last few weeks' changes for multiple days, but we have a time frame in which to work. Previous versions of this course revealed that the size of one's body has a huge impact on self-esteem and social life that cuts across the mortal and mage world in ways that are deeper than other biases. I know that some of you are from mortal or mage cultures where one body form is more ideal than others, so these changes can be more shocking."

I almost shrug, but I control myself by pulling my hands closer together on my desktop. One of my problems has always been that I don't look much like my grandmother and I can't remember enough about my mother to really judge if I should be shorter and thinner, taller and wider, or some other combination. Except for supermodels, who are valued for that exotic—a word we are not allowed to say out loud in class—look from being interracial, I don't have a lot of physical role models. I know that I don't have the same body shape as either a boy or girl, and there seems to be a lot of variety out there even among my own classmates.

We all grow very quiet as the short questionnaire and our collective answers are revealed. The teachers keep saying that this is all to be expected and that we aren't bad, but I know from the look that Brizo gives me at one point that I'm not the only one ashamed of our answers. Our previous such quizzes let us think we were open-minded and accepting; now we see we all have some nasty thoughts about what others look like.

"We're going to start with being overweight, and it will not be by a small amount." We all hold our breath as the professor continues. "While an extra twenty kilos—that's about forty-four pounds—might not seem like a lot, given the rate of obesity in the region you all live in, this will happen in moments, rather than gradually over months or years."

"If you are already that much overweight, your body will fall down into the average range for your sex, ethnicity, and height," Tutor Lubit adds after a look from the professor, who is now taking over the display.

"Let's go over some of the physical differences you may feel," Professor Russo says.

After a good twenty minutes, we break into pairs to talk about what we might expect. "I put on some weight last week; that was freaky enough," I confess to Brizo when we turn toward each other.

"I didn't have that, but then, I'm always like this," she says, motioning to her ample body. Before I can say anything else, she quickly asks, "By some measurements I'm overweight, but that just helps with the swimming, and a lot of that is muscle too. I don't know if I'm gonna change or not."

"Or how much," I point out, referring to one of the bits of information the teacher gave us. For many of us, our weight isn't much over or under, and we'll adjust into that category. I don't want to guess how much Brizo might change, because assuming her weight is normally rude.

"I think you'll definitely go up, Blake," Brizo points out. "And go down for sure next week, as I will."

"I'm glad you don't think I'm super thin or fat," I chuckle, then blush, because I've already made a poor choice by voicing my biases, but my seatmate doesn't react.

"I guess I'll go up about twenty pounds or so; how much of a difference can that really make?" she replies with a chuckle of her own. By the end of the class period, only a handful of us are smiling when we leave the room.

No one at the drama club table comments on what my new body looks like. No one says anything about the fact that I've taken the same food I'd normally take when offered these same choices in the lunch line. They just greet me and then go back to their conversations. *Am I the only sophomore in our club who eats at this time?* I look up and down the table and see no one else who has changed. *Why haven't I noticed this before?* I can't be the only sophomore in the entire group.

I look around the dining room and spot another of my classmates I know from drama sitting with the science geeks. Yes, he's in the stage craft department, where I was last year, but we didn't have much else in common, so I didn't really pay much attention to his name. I need to start learning my classmates' names.

I see another member of the drama club from my year at the table where a lot of the academically focused students meet up to ignore each other while they eat and read or do homework. She's one of the minor actors with a bit part who joined this year. Those of us in costuming haven't even taken the measurements of the supporting cast yet. She looks up over her book, and our eyes lock. I feel my face heat up, so I turn back to my food.

I just stare at the food but don't touch it, even though I feel hungry.

I almost jump out of my seat when I feel a hand on mine. I look up to see Efemena's rainbow-colored eyes staring into mine. "What?" I croak out softly.

"You should eat," she tells me. "Remember, all of this"—she makes a gesture toward my body—"isn't affecting how much food you need to eat. If you think you need to compensate, that's gonna make this week tough. I remember from two years ago."

Normally I think of Efemena as arrogant, so I'm surprised at how kind her words seem right now. I nod and cut off a bite of roast. Only after I've eaten it does she let my hand go. "I passed out on day three because I simply stopped eating," she whispers to me. "I'd like to avoid seeing others go through that if possible."

"Oh, yeah, that could be a problem," I agree.

My phone signals a text message from my grandmother, causing several people at the table glance in my direction. I take it out and read: *Just checking in. I know this is your lunchtime. Just let me know you are doing well.*

She didn't say anything about *True You* before I left this morning, only her normal wishing me a good day and asking if I needed any pocket cash or lunch money. Grandma hasn't checked on me via text since the first day of classes.

My phone goes off again: *Blake? Are you eating?*

I close my eyes for a second then text back: *Yes. Beef roast with veggies and sorbet.*

Grandma texts back: *I know what not to make, then. Have a good afternoon, dear.*

I put my phone away and slowly finish my food, finding that it doesn't taste quite right.

"I hate this," Seb groans as he slides down the bus seat as far as he can. I look across the aisle at him and frown.

He was sulky all day, but then that's how everyone from *True You* was today. Victoria reaches across and pinches his arm, and he hisses in response. "You don't remember what this is like," he counters.

A few rows ahead of us, more of our classmates are dealing with the same changes, but they are ignoring everything and everyone around them, staring out the windows. Several times I caught someone looking at me, and we both looked away. If I thought last week's minor weight change was bad, today I feel short of breath and very conscious of my body in ways I'm not used to. Luckily, our uniforms change with the spells, so our clothes still fit. *Oh, no, my clothes at home won't fit!*

"Why a full week?" Seb complains.

"To help you build empathy, idiot," Victoria tells him. Her body is a bit fuller than a lot of girls', but in all the right places. If anyone ever called her fat, she'd probably curse them or punch them in the face. Sitting next to her, even with the aisle between us, I feel self-conscious again about my in-between status. Even with the extra weight, I'll come across as androgynous unless I use clothing to send other signals.

"Like *your* empathy?" Seb growls back.

The mortals frown and toss a few concerned looks at us. At the next stop one of them pauses by Seb and glares down at him. "Skip lunch a few times and maybe you can get a hot babe like that," the jerk says before turning to wink at Victoria and ignore me, Haydar, and Eva, all of us within a row of each other. None of our previous *True You* changes got us all to sit so close together, but then again, none of our previous changes were this aligned with all of us changing in the same way.

Victoria gives him a cold smile but says nothing. We were at Reinholdt when Victoria took this class, but I can't seem to recall how Seb reacted to her changes.

The few classmates whose bodies decreased in weight, like Maxima and Oswine, may have been smiling when they left class, but whenever I caught their eyes, they acted the same as the rest of us. I thought they'd be happy, but they weren't acting cheerful when I saw them around the school. Neither of them are on this bus. Oswine is a jock in several sports, so he's probably at the school gym or something. Maxima is picked up by a private car at the end of each day, though where they go, I don't know; she isn't part of any extracurricular activities, and other than the one class, I don't see her much during the day.

Our bus stops, and Seb bolts for the doors as quickly as he can. As he walks away, Victoria says something very softly under her breath. We all hear a young masculine voice cry out as Seb tumbles from the bus onto the sidewalk.

The bus driver scrambles out of his seat and goes to help. Victoria motions to our schoolmates who live in this general area, and we exit via the side door. "Walking won't hurt any of us," Victoria says as we four follow her.

I'm shocked by what I see outside the bus. Seb is getting off the ground, and the jerk who insulted him is standing there screaming. As we walk past the jerk, we can see that his shoes have burst, revealing enlarged, swollen feet. "Looks like a nasty allergy," the bus driver is saying while a woman is pulling off the broken sneakers.

"What kind of allergy makes your feet swell up?" the jerk replies. He's too focused on his deformity and the woman's care of him to pay us much attention.

"That was risky," Eva says softly as she catches up to me and Victoria, leaving the boys to follow behind.

"He didn't have to touch my brother; he triggered that punishment by his own cruelty."

"Still, risky to do that sort of thing out here," Eva repeats, but I only bite my lower lip to keep from saying what I feel about it. *Would I be brave enough to do that? No.* But I'm glad that Victoria did it for her brother, even if they do seem to dislike each other most of the time.

"It will wear off once he's taken a bath or soaked his feet. They'll suspect it was something he stepped on or maybe the laundry detergent. Don't worry about it," Victoria assures us. "Surely you defended yourself the past few weeks when you got to enjoy the racism of mortals," she adds with a chuckle.

Eva throws me a look but says nothing as we walk along. Eva is more than just a cheerleader. This year she's a reporter for the school newspaper. She's done a series of reflection pieces since starting *True You* that are well done. If any of us or our classmates had been using magic outside of school, would she report on that and risk getting us all into trouble? I can't ask right now, but her look suggests she might hide that. I haven't been doing retaliatory magic, but I do routinely use simple spells to hide my body's limitations or enhance my feminine features.

"I read your articles about all of this," I tell Eva with a wave down at my own larger body.

Eva smiles, and Victoria gives me a slight bow of her head. "I was surprised to learn that it had been a decade since the paper covered the class," Eva tells us, "and then it was all stats and history. I know we can't talk specifics with the frosh but warding that part of the paper turned out to be relatively easy."

"If we could do that for our shows, we could do *Oh! Calcutta!* for the spring play," Victoria chuckles.

"What's that?" Eva asks.

"It's a mortal play where the majority of the cast is naked for most of the show," I answer. "No one wants to see that," I add, with a frown directed at Victoria.

Eva makes a strange face like she's eaten something horrid, then shudders. At the corner she and the Hileses head in one direction, while Haydar and I continue toward our own homes. Haydar jogs a few steps to catch up and walk alongside me, and I let him.

We walk silently for a few minutes, and then Haydar asks, "Blake, is this class making you, I don't know, freak out a bit?"

My confirmative reply catches in my throat. This could be an opening I've been dreaming about for years: someone I could share my secret with who might understand. I glance at Haydar and take in his glasses and extra-large satchel before returning my gaze to his face, where he's just starting to show some fuzz above his upper lip. No, he wouldn't understand. Even the biggest nerd in our class is becoming a man, his body undergoing normal changes like a typical teenager.

"Not freak out, but it can be a bit weird," I offer in as firm a voice as I can muster.

"Yeah, weird," he repeats. After a few moments of silence, he continues, "My parents told me some strange stuff last week about their time in this class."

"Like what?" It must be nice to have someone at home who cares enough to discuss this in relationship to their own pasts. I feel like I have to pull hard or be tricky about getting any information. My grandmother has been generally supportive, as is my uncle, aside from a few slips about my hair or my gender. Mostly, they just ask how my day was, listen to what I might say, and then ask about homework or the theater preparations. If I'm struggling, they're more likely to join in my attempts to see the positive by adding in their own praise or changing how they look. Anything but offer information about themselves or my parents. I'm curious if Haydar's family is actually doing more or if I'm being overly sensitive, as mass media tells me that teens tend to be, so I press, "If you can share it, that is. I'm happy to listen."

Haydar stops right where he is, so I do as well. His face changes subtly but visibly, suggesting that he's struggling with different emotions. It's rather refreshing to see a guy have more emotions than angry, goofy, or turned on, which seem to be Seb's default settings now.

After a moment Haydar meets my eyes, so I smile and nod firmly. "This will stay between us, I promise."

His face relaxes, and he begins softly. "They knew each other in school, and they were …" He swallows and looks around. I mimic his glances but see no one near us. "They were both girls at the start of the term. My dad liked girls—identified as a lesbian, even though that was real rough to do back then at the beginning of the twentieth century. My mom was only attracted to boys except for my dad; it was confusing for her. They told me that their affection for each other influenced the final spell of the class."

"That's romantic," I say, but Haydar only shakes his head. "I've seen your parents around," I go on. "Everyone can see how much they love each other. That love is part of the reason they're faith leaders in both worlds," I point out. Here in Brooklyn they head a local new-age temple that connects to a magic temple with a gateway between our realms in the middle of the building. We don't attend, but I've seen them in both mortal and enchanted news stories over the years. They are well respected and even get mortal grants to attend religion conferences around the world multiple times a year. They aren't cult leaders or televangelists, no matter what some tabloids might claim.

"Don't you get it, Blake? This class is supposed to reveal the true us—the unique individual—not be directed by emotions or current events in either realm. But if my parents are correct, then that's a lie. Can you think what might happen if one of us was having a bad morning before that final class? Who knows what we could end up as, and we'd be stuck with it," Haydar hissed as he looked around nervously again.

My heart is pounding now, and I can feel my larger body start to sweat in fear. On one hand, I've been suspecting that some force beyond ourselves might influence that final spell—maybe the Fates, as Grandmother says, or some magical foresight—but I hadn't thought about our emotional state. I shake my head a few times, and Haydar's eyes widen. No, this course is going to make me right, correct the error of my body, fix me on the most basic level. It has to, or I'll have this secret forever.

Haydar looks like he might pass out, so I grab his hand. "It will be fine. You and I will make an appointment to walk from that bus stop every day and talk about what we're thinking. That way neither of us will mess up the final spell with overactive fears."

"You'd do that for me? I thought you and Seb were, you know."

I blink, then laugh. "Haven't you noticed what a jerk he's become since summer vacation?" I counter.

Haydar just shrugs and says, "He's into sports; isn't that pretty standard for those guys, mortal or mage?"

That isn't the answer I want to hear, so I frown and start marching down our shared street. He catches up with me, but I don't say another word. "I'm sorry, Blake, I know this sort of thing is important to girls, but I'm so busy with my classes and my family that I'm not really into relationships yet," he offers.

I pause when he calls me a girl, and I feel less angry. "I shouldn't be into relationships either," I reply. "I should be focused on our classwork, magic, the drama club, or even my family. But I guess that's just girls for you, right?"

"I guess. The girls I hang out with are mostly into science and tech, magic or not, and they couldn't care less about us guys unless we can help them find a programming error or the like," Haydar admits. "I think you may be the first normal girl who has said more than one sentence to me outside of class this year."

I pull my arms closer to my body because I really want to hug him right now for making my day—heck, my week—with his words. Instead I settle for a smile and say, "We're agreed we'll walk and talk each day, then?"

"Yeah, yeah, we'll be sounding boards for each other." As we stroll, we continue to converse about some of the other changes we've been through, though I carefully avoid saying anything that might make him think I'm anything but that normal girl.

Too soon, I can see my house and then Haydar's only a few driveways down. I don't realize I haven't thought about Seb again until my uncle asks about class at dinner.

It isn't unusual for me to wear my school uniform to dinner most nights and then to do my homework in my room unless Grandmother wants my help with something. So it takes Grandma a few days before she investigates what's going on by coming to my room.

I stare at the manifested goat's head as it bleats out, "Graaaaandmother at the door," a second time. I'm sitting at my desk, doing some reading ahead for a course to keep my mind off the fact that my body feels less like me than any of the previous changes. It's like I can feel every breath and movement when it wasn't noticeable to me before.

"Blake, dear, I just want to check on you," Grandmother calls through the goat's mouth.

I take a deep breath and remind myself that she is going to be supportive. "You may come in," I say out loud.

Grandmother comes inside slowly and then straightens up when she sees that I'm still in my uniform. She says nothing, then nods once and walks over to my closet. She opens it, and I sit there silently as she pulls out one of my favorite shirts, then a pair of my comfortable pants.

"They won't fit," I start to say, but she tosses me one of her looks that means any argument is a waste of time.

She keeps pulling out clothes until she has five sets in her arms. She puts these on the bed and motions for me to come to her. "Didn't they teach you the attunement spell yet?" She tsks as she hands me a sweater.

"Attunement? I mean, we cast that on our school journals last year, and we cast them on our textbooks for each class," I offer as I hold up the sweater. I can tell it won't fit well, and I just want to cry, but I swallow hard instead.

"I'm sure we were taught this; it's so basic," Grandmother sighs as she steps back to look at me. "Well, we're in the privacy of our home, so just don't do this elsewhere, and it will be fine. Repeat these gestures and words on the item you're holding," she instructs me.

I blink. Other than a few spells I've overheard, or the ones she's shown me involving her healing arts—some of which I'd say were more vanity than health—she's never actually taught me magic. The schools are supposed to do that, so lines of specializations are family linked, or some such thing we were taught last year.

The words are simple, though I'm careful with the pronunciation, and the hand movements are basically pushing the clothing against my body, making sure to have my hand touch each part. I flip the sweater over when told and repeat the phrases and strokes of my hand.

"Now put it on," Grandmother commands.

After a blush and a "Grandma, turn around then" from me, she does so. I take off my school vest and put it on top of my blazer that is over the back of my chair. I take off my shirt and wince at my too-tight bra beneath. It isn't school issued, so it's been uncomfortable even on the widest setting. I've stretched my undies out as well, but I've only washed the one pair in the morning while showering so I can't damage other pairs. My hairdryer has been helpful with that as well.

The sweater doesn't visibly change, but it also doesn't feel tight at all against my body. I turn and look at myself in the mirror. I'm still not happy with what I see, but I don't look bad either. "Will this work on all my clothes?"

"Yes, yes; before we all became obsessed with clothing, it was necessary. I had three dresses for most of my life," Grandmother tells me.

"Thank you, thank you!" I gush as I turn around and cross the distance between us as fast as I can. She almost steps back when I pull her into a hug, but after a moment she relaxes and returns my embrace.

"They should be teaching this," Grandma says softly after we stop hugging and take a couple of steps back.

"But you taught me, Gran. You taught me," I say with tears at the corners of my eyes.

She blushes and turns away with a wave of her hand. "You do a few more while I watch to make sure it goes well, then I'll let you finish these on your own."

I grip the sweater with a huge grin on my face and nod happily for a second before calming myself so I can cast correctly. Once I have a pair of pants, a skirt, and a dress properly attuned, Grandmother leaves me to work on the rest. I'm up far too late, but I manage to attune every piece of my wardrobe to my body.

Dear Journal,

I always thought that fat people were taunted mercilessly, but the thing I'm noticing is how ignored I am when I'm out in the mortal world. Don't get me wrong, I don't want some loser insulting me at the bus stop or at the grocery store when I go help Grandma shop, but this was just weird. I feel like people make an effort to walk around me or look at me funny.

I know about the feeling of people looking at you. I feel it all the time when I dare to wear anything that isn't my uniform or really feminine. I didn't feel it that much, though when I did, it felt different. It was more a sense of pity. Not that I'm saying I can read people's feelings. I can barely figure out what I'm feeling half the time.

The thing is, I'm not huge. I'm 40 pounds more, which still feels enormous, even though I see a lot of others much bigger than me. As I wrote that, I realized how much I notice about people's size. I was feeling proud that I wasn't as big as the man buying beer or that woman trying to handle three kids in the store.

I think this is the empathy lesson this week is supposed to be teaching us. Now I feel like a jerk for all the times I've chosen another aisle to walk down or stepped around someone a bit more than necessary.

Can the Solstice get here soon so I can have a break from all these changes?

"You don't look good," Seb tells me when we meet for lunch on Monday.

I give him an up and down glare. "You look emaciated yourself," I reply with a forced laugh. Many of us do look a bit too thin today, and we're going to need to cope with it all week long. Our uniforms adjusted, so really, I don't feel much different.

"It's different for guys," Seb continues as we go to the line to pick out our food.

"How so?" I shoot back. "Girls are judged by what we look like all the time."

"Yeah but being thin is something you're supposed to be. You know what I mean," he replies to my pointed look. "The mortal realm is all about how fragile girls should look, not that they should be in my opinion."

I'm hurt that he's talking about general girls and not including me with them, but I hope I'm just being too paranoid about that. The truth is, when I looked in the mirror, I saw a young boy starting back, so I asked Brizo if she had any extra makeup. It turns out that, as part mermaid, she can't wear makeup because of her skin, so I had to ask Eva for hers, and she had ample supplies to share. Grandmother won't let me wear makeup or even buy it yet, so Eva helped me apply some as well. I toss my head back, hoping Seb will notice my more feminine looking face, but he just keeps talking about boys.

"A guy is supposed to be big and strong—something I've not been blessed with naturally, so this just sucks. At least last week I could literally throw my weight around, and once I started doing that, I felt pretty good."

I pause at his words and let my reply tumble out of my mouth. "Is that why you've been so moody? You think you aren't big enough?"

"Blake!" he hisses back as he steps closer. "Table for two please," he suggests as his eyes dart around. I follow his gaze, but I don't see anyone looking at us.

Once we have our trays of food and are at a two-person table, Seb starts to eat. I wait a few seconds then clear my throat loudly. "Is that why you've been a jerk? Because you think you're too small because you're a boy?"

"Certainly today," Seb counters, but his tone is too light to be real, so I narrow my eyes at him.

After a moment, I cross my arms over my chest and nearly cry at how it feels like there is almost nothing there anymore. I didn't have a lot to start with, but this is just—no, no. I growl to snap myself of it, and that makes Seb's eyes go wide. "Tell me, or I'll say really loudly how tiny you are, and people can think I'm talking about particular body parts," I whisper back to cover my own worries.

"You wouldn't … you would," he says after a second of my continued stare. "I thought that over the summer I'd go through a growth spurt."

"You did! You're like a half foot taller now," I point out. In fact, I just noticed last week that Seb was finally a bit taller than me.

"Yeah, well, the muscle didn't come with the height. With all these class changes, I can't seem to bulk up."

"I don't think boys automatically get a lot of muscles," I start to say, but Seb leans closer to the table, so I stop.

"That's what I said. I've been trying to bulk up. Adding in weights, working out with the teams, trying their protein shakes, even using the family gym at home. But when I'm just myself, I don't seem to be any different."

"Maybe height comes before muscle," I offer, but honestly I don't know. Other than research to figure out how certain parts of me may work, I've been focused on becoming a real girl. "I mean, most teens aren't as muscled as adult men, right?"

"Yes, but," his eyes glance elsewhere, so I follow his gaze. Burim again.

"You shouldn't be comparing yourself to Mister Jock," I state, and Seb's gaze swings back to me. "You should just wait and see what you are by the end of our class."

"Probably—that's what Victoria and my parents say. I mean, you put on makeup today, so you know it isn't easy to just go with these changes."

He noticed the makeup. *Wait, he knows I did it because I'm not happy with what this loss of weight has made me look like.* That's not what I wanted to achieve. After lunch, I go wash my face. The next time I see Eva, I give her the little kit back with a "thank you" and use my grandmother as an excuse for not keeping it.

Dear Journal,

I thought that having more weight was difficult for a full week, but now I'm freezing. Uncle Delmar fussed over me the entire time after I got home and before he left for work. He tried to get me to eat more, even after Grandmother reminded him that it won't change my body because of the spell. Hot drinks did help, so Grandma kept those coming my way. When I was fatter, they didn't seem to be that worried, and I realized that I was mostly being ignored by everyone I met in the mortal world.

I glanced in the mirror when I got home and nearly cried. I can see my bones, yuck! I thought I was skinny before, but I'll never complain about that again.

Some of our classmates were so happy after the morning's rituals, but I've been feeling ill all day long. I can't even look at my fingers without cringing.

On the upside, if I never show mage talent and I turn out like this, I can become a supermodel. They still go for the hyper-thin look in some parts of the world, and mixed heritage, or what the mortals call "exotic," seems all the rage when I check out their magazines. Not that I read them a lot—just to keep on top of what I should look like.

No, I can't end up thinner. I look even more androgynous than normal. Seb didn't say anything to me at all today, though he did shoot me a few sad looks. At least Haydar, Eva, or one of the theater members stayed close to me all day. Eva even lent me one of the sweaters she brought with her because her mother warned her about the temperature issue.

Wish Grandma or Uncle had warned me.

Every day for a week, Haydar and I have gotten off the bus a stop early where the Hileses and Eva normally exit. At first, the other three tried to catch up with us, but they stayed on the bus after Victoria asked point-blank in drama club, "Are you dating Haydar now?". For some reason, Seb has stopped talking to me altogether again, though he keeps looking at me.

Back to Haydar. We walk, we talk about the rest of our day outside of True You. Slowly we've started to share more information and get to know each other better, but I never feel safe enough to tell him about my mismatched features under my trousers.

The next unit starts soon. I just hope nothing odd happens with the spells because of what I am.

Chapter 6: Everybody Changes

"Welcome back!" Professor Russo and Tutor Lubit greet us as we return to class on Monday. This is it, the topic I've been both dreading and yearning for: Gender and Sexuality. These two weeks are our last before the Solstice break. We'll still have another term to go for the spring, but I'm hoping that for the break I can be simply a normal girl.

"First, turn in your journals," Professor Russo orders. The twenty of us pass our journals forward to Tutor Lubit, who gives them the box treatment before passing them back to their owners.

I set the journal to one side and take out the course textbook. My hands are shaking, but when I glance left and right, I see that my nearest classmates' hands are fumbling or shaking too. *What would they be afraid of?* There will be sex changes for a rare student at the term's end, but that only accounts for maybe one student in our section, according to our textbook. The book also claims that only a few of us will be strictly straight, gay, or lesbian, because most mages are bisexual. The expectation is to reproduce, something I don't think I can do, but I'm not sure. I have my period by now, but it's light and erratic—a couple months can pass with nothing, then I'll bleed for two weeks. The intersex website says that reproductive functions vary a lot across people like me. With any luck, or the blessing of the Fates, I won't need that website come summer. I feel my face flush at that hope.

Sure, my classmates and other students talk about who's hot and who's not—most of what I'm privy to happens at theater meetings and rehearsals—but no one really discusses sex. Sexual violence is rampant back in Brooklyn and the rest of the mortal realm, but when both predator and prey could easily damage or even kill each other with magic, you learn to be careful. The statistics in our textbook for our people is nearly zero. When the target retaliates and the attacker escapes, the Central Council sends its people to hunt the rapist down. Luckily a pregnancy among mages requires the consent of both parties or the equivalent of a medical intervention.

I once asked Grandmother if she's ever used that sort of magic to help mortal couples or women. "That would be against our laws," she simply said, which didn't really answer my question, as usual.

"Let's review what we've done thus far. Lubit, please do the honors," Professor Russo directs. I've got a few minutes, then, before the nightmare starts.

"I'm delighted to do so, Professor," the tutor replies. He waves his hand, and the lights dim as the projection he conjures comes down in front of the room. I try to focus on what he's telling us, but I've pre-read the chapter, and my mind won't stop churning. I just know these spells won't work properly on me. It must work on me. It has to fix everything that's wrong with me. *What if it can't? What if it won't?*

To pull my thoughts together, I watch the Professor go back to her chair. She looks over us all, but I know her gaze lingers on me. I wish I could vanish, but we won't learn that until next year, and even then, not everyone will be skilled at it. I tried to claim I was sick this morning, but Grandmother saw right through it—since abjuration is her specialty. The professor's gaze returns to the tutor, and I feel myself relax just a touch.

"What a waste of our time," complains Seb after we leave class. I look around, but no one else is nearby, the other students evidently fleeing class today. Surprised, I let him walk next to me. Apparently, I'm still okay to complain to—at least it's some type of conversation. "An entire period going over what we've done in the past five weeks. I know what feels right for me," he declares, lightening his hair, skin, and eyes as we walk.

I pull him into a side hallway, hissing, "Are you crazy? You know we aren't supposed to do that outside of class. What if a frosh saw you? They're freaked out enough with learning that magic really works."

"You're such a prissy, Blake," Seb tells me, but he slides back to his default form. "It's only an illusion," he points out.

When did he get so good at illusions? Where did he learn them at all? Did his family teach him? Is that his talent? I don't ask, because that would only draw attention to the fact that I have no idea what mine is. I just roll my eyes and pull my blazer tighter around my body. "What's happened to you? Ever since summer you've been ..." I wave my hand at him, trying to think of the words.

"More assertive? More a man?" he offers with what looks like a sneer. "It's called puberty—you should try it sometime."

I frown and look down at my shoes. *Been there, done that—have the mini pads to prove it.* I don't tell him that. Instead I feel frozen in place. I want to yell at him, to remind him of how little muscle mass he's put on, but that feels mean. Just because he's being mean, that doesn't force me to be the same, Grandmother would say.

He must sense my discomfort, because Seb touches my arm lightly and mutters, "I'm sorry, Blake. I know you feel self-conscious around the other girls because you aren't as ... developed." I can't believe he actually makes boob gestures in front of his chest as he says it. *Why am I here with this jerk?*

"Blake! Don't be like that!" he calls after me as I stomp toward the chorus room where I can get away from him.

Professor Nudd Cepko nods at me when I walk in and take my position for triple trio practice. I'm positioned in the middle tier, because I'm not as tall or as short as some of the others, and my voice can cover a wider scale—even dipping into the tenor range. "Your voice is a musical wonder," he told me last year when I stupidly showed up for tryouts. If only he knew why I can sing in a wide range, he wouldn't use the term *wonder* anymore.

Two course blocks later, Seb is holding an empty chair for me in the cafeteria, but I just toss my head, sending my dark brown ponytails swinging. Instead, I go sit with Victoria and the rest of the artsy clique, as I have been for most of the term. I don't need to hang with Jerky Boy.

The half dozen of them smile and make room for me to sit down. I use their greetings as a shield against the feeling of Seb's glare.

"Is my brother's charm particularly vile today?" Victoria asks me, earning laughter from all of us.

"He's just not who he was last year," I reply softly.

"That happens to boys. Maybe he'll learn something in these next two weeks." I look up at Victoria, then at the other junior and the two frosh, before I look back at her, trying to silently urge her to be quiet. The headmaster told us horror stories about students who tried to learn magic too early. Older students can talk about their experiences with younger ones only if the underclass student is currently in that course. "We can hope," she adds.

"I did," Wigheard replies. "Oh, I know you think I've always been a gallant, but that wasn't so until after the first term of my sophomore year."

The two frosh exchange looks but don't dare ask. I'm grateful that none of the others expand on that. I don't want to get into trouble, if it might get me kicked out of *True You. Especially* if it might get me kicked out of that class.

Instead, we return to our ongoing debate about which of the ten actors who tried out we think should make the cut for our autumn spectacular. Wigheard, of course, is already the lead act, so he'll have a voice in the decisions. None of us have final say, though generally Professor Hermans takes our analysis seriously when she makes the final cuts.

The show won't involve much more work for me and the costumes and makeup team because it's basically a chance for our most talented people to showcase themselves with scenes from previous productions. A few alterations and some help with makeup is all that will be required. The play was a success, and I learned a lot from it, but I'm really struggling with finding costumes and makeup as interesting as I did sets and lighting last year.

I glance over at the jock table but don't see Seb. I try to be casual as I look around, then I spot him alone at a table for two. He gives me a slight smile when he sees me looking, so I turn back to my own table. Let him sit for a while by himself.

I don't have to hide from Seb the rest of the day, because he decides to hang out with the jocks when he's not in class. *Why do boys always have to be pushing and poking each other right out in the hallways? Yet they are all laughing. Is Seb looking at the team captain with his weird, wide eyes?* I turn away, my cheeks warm. He has new friends and doesn't need freaky me. That's fine. Happens throughout high school, even in the mortal world. Television, books, and movies tell me so. Victoria told me so. It still hurts to see him with others in the halls between courses. Yet when we have the same course, I just walk past him to my assigned seat.

All this drama outside of theater club makes me exhausted by the time I'm back home. I ignore Seb and the others on the rail and subway lines, tuning them out with the music from my headphones. I even cross an extra street walking back home just to put more distance between Haydar and myself. I feel a twinge of guilt about that and glance back, but he's put his own headphones on and has stopped to look at something on a neighborhood bulletin board.

Grandmother and Uncle Delmar are both at home when I arrive. "Hey, Blake, you look just like you did this morning! How was school?" my uncle asks me as he lays the newspaper on the dining room table. Grandmother is finishing up chicken and waffles, the smell filling the room and making my stomach growl.

His question makes my head hurt, but I just smile and set my backpack on the entry stand, which transports it to my bedroom. "Courses are courses, but we did narrow down the actors for the spectacular," I tell them as I go to the half bath to wash up.

Grandmother is standing next to the stovetop filling up a bottle when I come back out. "Do you have a headache? Cramps?" she asks, and I can feel my face heat up when my uncle chuckles.

"Just hungry," I huff as I take a seat at the table.

"You know you don't need to be embarrassed with us," Grandmother tries to reassure me, but I really wish it were summer so I would be who I'm supposed to be—or just disappear. You finally get your period two years later than your mother, and the entire family has to know about it. Seb has no idea what it's like. Part of me hopes he'll be the one to switch sex at the end of the second term so he can really understand.

"Boy trouble, girl trouble?" my uncle asks.

I want to say both—trouble with other students and within myself—but instead I reply, "Some people turn into jerks in high school."

"True," he replies.

Grandmother makes a face at his unhelpful reply as she finishes up and sets a bottle aside. Now I can see it's a syrup bottle, meaning that she's made it from scratch. "Sometimes when we like someone and they don't like us back, or they don't know how to express their feelings, it seems like they're being jerks," she suggests as she directs the platters of food and the bottle to the table. This is such an American thing to eat that I'm always shocked and pleased when she prepares it. *Did she make it thinking that I'd need comfort food tonight?*

"You like someone at school, then?" my uncle pushes before he takes in an exaggerated breath of the aromas from the table.

"Me?" I can't think of what else to say. Do I like Seb like a boyfriend? Maybe … but I also like others. I feel my face heating up at the horror of talking about any of this, so I blurt out, "I'm very focused on schoolwork right now. I don't have time for that!"

My guardians exchange a silent look, and then Grandmother says, "You know, some of my mage clients are worse than my mortal ones."

The conversation around the table turns to lighter topics about Grandmother's clients or the mortal letters to the editor that my uncle reads out loud to make us roll our eyes.

Before he leaves, my uncle puts a hand on one of my shoulders, as he has for years. This time he puts a hand on my other shoulder as well. "My strong Blake," he says in an oddly softer tone before tossing out, "Don't do anything I wouldn't do," in his joking manner.

Grandmother is also looking at me oddly when I turn around, but she just huffs, and before she starts doing the dishes by hand, orders, "Homework, then I'll give you some tea and biscuits."

Dear Journal,

That's it! Seb and I are no longer friends.

He was a real jerk, and I know I've written that before, but today was the final insult. He can have the sports jerks if he wants. I have other friends.

So why do I keep trying with him? Just a weird old habit. Not like we went to school together in the mortal world for most of our lives, just two years. We mostly played in the neighborhood and at mage events our families were at. I couldn't have stayed his friend if he knew what happened back in London, if he knew my secret.

I wish I had a good friend.

Oh, no! I left Haydar behind. Will he be pissed? Probably not, he's such an easygoing guy. What if he isn't a guy in the end? Will that matter to me? I don't even know what I'm going to be.

Haydar would say that we'll all be our true selves ... what does that even mean?

I wish I knew chronokinesis so I could skip ahead to the end of next term and just be normal, whatever that is for me.

"I didn't mean to ignore you," I blurt out at the bus stop when I see Haydar the next morning. I didn't see him at our normal one, so I walked to the next, hoping I'd catch him. We've been walking the extra distance to chat first thing, and I'm relieved he's kept that routine. I offer him the wrapped scones I took from my grandmother's breakfast platter. "I didn't make them, so they're safe to eat," I quickly explain when he unwraps one and gives me an odd look.

He breaks into a laugh and takes a bite. "Not into domestic arts, huh? Me neither, though I'm a bit of a neat freak," he tells me after that one bite. "I'll save the rest for later."

I nod several times and look at my shoes. Then he nudges me, so I look up at him again. "Nothing for you to apologize for. Today's a big day for you girls—must be scary."

"What's scary?" Eva's voice makes us both look up. She's arrived dressed in trousers instead of her usual skirt.

"Sex change," Haydar states.

"Thus these," Eva replies as she waves one hand down the side of her body. "Figured I'd go with these rather than having my junk swinging around under a skirt."

I note that her comment makes Haydar's cheeks flush, so I bump his arm lightly before chiming in, "I think kilts are okay even over here now, right?"

"Probably, but you'd need to talk to our 'pop culture' reporter," Eva says, using her fingers to make air quotes around the title. "I'll be doing the boys' routines in cheer this weekend, I guess. That can't be too hard. Stand, clap in time, yell a few things. I doubt they'll let me toss up anyone to catch."

"Do you get tossed up?" Haydar asks.

Eva makes a pained face at him then shakes her head. "You pay no attention at all. No, no, I'm in a different position on the squad."

"That would scare me," Haydar says. Both Eva and I look at each other, then blink when we've deciphered what he's talking about.

"Me, too," I tell him. "Keep my feet on the ground, please."

"I can do my own flips, and I'm not teeny, so no tossing of me," Eva explains. She looks at her phone for a moment, then around at the small gathering of folks waiting. "I thought Seb might be here, since there're no morning practices today," she tells us with a shrug.

I frown slightly. *Have they been chatting like Haydar and I have been?* That makes my stomach feel off, but I'm not angry, more annoyed that I didn't know that about his schedule.

"I thought most of the teams had meets or whatever until the Solstice," Haydar wonders aloud.

"Not soccer. They're finished for the term, and I think Seb hasn't figured out if he wants to continue to manage for the second term," Eva tells us.

He's thinking of quitting sport? Now nothing makes sense.

"Maybe he changed his mind," Haydar offers as the bus pulls up.

"Boys changing their minds? That never happens," Eva teases. I let her move closer so she can follow me up the steps into the bus. We grab a trio of side seats with us two girls on one end.

Right before the door closes, Seb slips aboard. He stares at us for a moment, then works his way to stand near the back door even though Eva waves at him. "Haven't you two made up yet?" she whispers to me.

Great. The entire school must be gossiping about our blowup yesterday. I ignore Seb as he stands there watching the three of us.

I want to disappear into my chair as *True You* starts the next morning. "You might all think you understand what being male means, but today, and for the rest of the week, we're going to explore what it means to each of us personally," Professor Russo says as we all take out our ritual kits.

"Boys," the professor continues, "you may think you have it easy this week, but each of you must take responsibility for your new brother and help him through the change. This means not just during classes you share, or here at the Institute, but also while you're out in the mortal and enchanted worlds. We've teamed you up based on the number of classes you share and your home address."

A card appears on my desktop with the name "Haydar Plank" written on it. I look up and exchange a nod with Haydar. Out of the corner of my eye I see Seb frowning at Eva, so he must be paired with her. *Why does he look disappointed? Was he hoping we'd be paired up?* Haydar and I have four classes together and, except for yesterday afternoon, we've continued our chats between the bus and home. Seb and I have only this one class and then history, where he's too busy trying to impress other boys or giving me the side-eye. I'm glad it's Haydar.

"Everyone stand up and take a flask," Professor Russo tells us as Tutor Lubit passes them out. Both she and the tutor also take a flask. We all repeat the words she says and copy her hand gestures over the flasks. "We will all drink them together. If you are already male, this will not affect you."

For a moment I pause, looking at the grayish liquid. *What will the potion make of me? Will it change me at all?* It has to; I'm not really male or female—I'm a freak—so this has to work.

I ignore the taste as I swallow. I can feel the magic pulsing down my throat to my stomach. The pinprick trails of fire race through my body. I close my eyes to try to calm myself. This feels painful compared to the previous potions and spells. There are groaning and moaning sounds around me, but I keep my eyes closed and try to figure out what is happening to my body.

"You may open your eyes now," says a voice that doesn't sound like the tutor's but is also not like our professor's. I don't know why it surprises me to see our professor as he is now. In a masculine form, Professor Russo is perhaps eight centimeters taller, with a fiery-red trimmed beard, and shorter, lighter hair still messily falling around her—no, *his*—squarer face. I'm just cataloging how his teaching uniform fits differently when I hear a giggle next to me.

I turn to see Seb looking at me. "Blake? Whoa, you got big," he says in a strange tone.

I'm turning my gaze down to my blazer and shirt, which are straining against my expanded shoulders and chest. The sleeves are revealing far too much skin. This isn't right; the clothing should have adjusted to our forms, as it did with the weight and height differences. The trousers seem tighter too, but before I can move a leg to check the length, I see Haydar's face in my line of sight.

"It will be okay, Blake," Haydar is telling me. "The school has extra uniforms. As Professor Russo told us, sometimes the changes are a bit more intense, and the attunements don't quite adjust, but that can be fixed. We'll get you some that fit better."

"Damn," I hear another voice say. I turn to see a boy in Maxima Garriland's place blinking back at me. "If that's pre-puberty … I am totally jealous."

"What is wrong with me?" I say too loudly.

Everyone is staring at me now. Haydar is holding out his hands, looking up at me, while Tutor Lubit, who has joined us, is standing eye to eye with me. Their voices all blur into noise as I try to move away, bumping into my desk. I feel like I can't breathe. I wish I could be anywhere but here.

Then everything turns a dark gray. I look around, but the room—my classmates, my teachers, my desk, everything—is gone.

Chapter 7: Between is Me

I feel around for the desks with my hands and kick out with my feet. I feel nothing except whatever passes for the ground here, supporting me, my too-big limbs, and their spastic movements.

"Hello?" I say, then shut my mouth. *That isn't my voice.* It's deep, rough. It sounds a lot like my uncle might if he lacked confidence. I swallow but feel nothing odd in my throat, though my hand confirms a slight bump on my neck where my vocal cords are.

I close my eyes and try to focus on the list of differences we've learned between masculine and feminine bodies. I use my hands as I run through the predicted changes. I expected a flat chest, but not this expansion across it and my shoulders. The ripping I heard must have been my blazer and shirt; the tears I feel in the fabric confirm it. *Why wouldn't the clothing spell have adjusted? Because I'm a freak.*

Luckily, the uniform trousers are loose-fitting, but even so, they feel tight. I pause and use my hands, withdrawing them once I feel the extra bits and pieces below. How could I forget about those? We went over that in class—hell, we went over it in fifth-grade mortal school.

I take a deep breath and try to get myself centered. I may have changed physically, but I can still think, right? I call out "Hello!" Only silence comes back. I try again, louder. My deeper voice doesn't even echo back. I stand up straight and yell as loudly as I can. Nothing.

I move my shoulders around, and the blazer rips more. I could take it off, but I'm worried about where I am. I fan out my fingers, then pause and wait. There doesn't seem to be any airflow, but I feel a chill over me. *Do boys get cold? I thought that was just girls.* Maybe it's just the rips in my clothing.

What would Seb do if he were here? No, I shouldn't be thinking about him. *What would Haydar do? What would Professor Russo do? What would my father do?* With that thought I'm sinking down to my knees. My sobs are terrifyingly jagged and deep, foreign and frightening, and they make me cry even more.

In a while, I have no more energy to cry, sitting alone in the gray cold. I have to lift up and readjust my position as pain shoots through my body. Damn it, so many more things to move around down there. In a few tries I'm seated with my knees spread as far as the tight trousers will allow without more ripping.

"Wait," I say as I get an idea. I still have my phone. I fumble in my blazer's inner pockets and pull it out. I start it up, and in a few moments, I can see more by the flashlight.

My hands are bigger, reminding me of my father's, and it takes a rough shake of my head to stop more crying. They remind me of my uncle's. Yeah, that's what they remind me of. *What would Uncle Delmar do if he were here?* I turn the light toward my clothing to check out the rips on the shoulders of my blazer and the strain in the waist of my trousers. Standing up confirms that I'm taller, my ankles and socks easily visible. My feet ache, and when I try to wiggle my toes I simply can't. I feel my face to find slightly rougher skin, but no beard or mustache. *Is that a blessing or a curse right now? How many boys at Reinholdt have facial hair? Few, very few, even among the seniors. Something isn't right about this. Story of my life.*

My phone isn't working right. There are little exclamation points in place of the data and Wi-Fi icons. I check and see my photos and stored books, but it won't connect to anything.

Did I do chronokinesis? Sweet! But why would everything be gray and cold? Is this like that old movie about the monsters that can eat the past? My uncle watched something like that a few weeks ago during his weekend off. I look around, holding my phone's flashlight outward, but see nothing other than gray. I strain to hear anything, picking up only the sound of my own heavy breathing.

If only I could figure out how to move back into the timeline before I freak out again, I could play it cool and be all, "This is what I was expecting." Then I could use my four days as a dude to really check it out—hang with Haydar and ask my uncle questions to make him blush or laugh, as he does with his invasive questioning of me.

Are you kidding me? I look down to my trousers, which are stretched even tighter. I can*not* be getting turned on by thinking about how my uncle annoys me. This body change is out of control. I don't even know where I *am* right now, and it's reacting like this? Girls joke about guys getting horny for anything, but *really*? I think of numbers, color coding for makeup, and anything else that bores me until my body is back to its unaroused state.

I take a few steps but have to stop because my feet hurt. "I'm no good if I can't run, just in case I'm not really alone," I say softly, looking around the gray. I untie my shoes but have to pull hard to get them off. My socks are stretched tight, but I work them around my ankles until they fit more comfortably. I tie the shoestrings together and hang my shoes around my neck.

Taking a few more steps, I call out, "Hello? Is anyone there? Don't be afraid of me even though I have this slightly scary voice now." I let the final words trail off. The surface below my feet is cool and hard, but not rough or dangerous ... probably.

"Blake!" I flinch at the sound of a muted feminine voice calling my name.

"Hello?" I call back as loudly as I can.

"Oh, good, you can hear me. This is Elfa Milford, the Reinholdt Counselor. I want you to try to determine where my voice is coming from and follow it back. Would you do that for me?"

"Yes! Keep talking!" I order as I start to turn slowly in a circle.

"You are doing great, Blake. You are one brilliant … student." The psychologist stumbles over what to call me, but I try to ignore that and focus on where the voice seems to be coming from. "We'll get you some better fitting clothes and a good meal. You have friends waiting here for you to get back."

Her chatter is not reassuring, but I don't say that out loud. Seeing the school counselor was the first thing that happened after the bullying in London. All he did was give me some pamphlet to read that wasn't even about being intersex. I hated those few weeks. I knew Milford wasn't the same person, but I didn't know if she was good at her job. Right now, I just need to get back to school, so I take a few short steps toward the voice, then take surer steps as she changes the topic to the weather. The gray fades back into Russo's classroom, and I have to shield my eyes with one hand, even though the lights aren't as bright as I remember them.

"There you are! That was very well done," Counselor Milford says. She's sitting on top of the desk in front of mine. I look down and see her hands holding my new bigger ones. "That was quite a show of talent!" she continues until Professor Russo's masculine form pushes into view.

"Thank you, Elfa; we'll bring Blake to your office in a few minutes," my professor says.

"That was neat!" said a voice off to my side. I turn to find Haydar standing next to me, his eyes bright and excited. "You completely disappeared! Scary, too, but mostly cool!"

"Yes, yes, let's all give Blake a few moments to reorient himself," our tutor says as he motions for Haydar and a few others to step back. I see Victoria and Wigheard among the small group of students from various classes. *Why are they all here? Where did they come from?* There are too many people staring at me. I start to see gray, and then something slaps around my wrist.

"That was a bit more of a change than you expected, eh?" Professor Russo chuckles, patting the magic dampener he's placed on me. I nod silently and let him take my arm to help me step down to the floor. "We all have different degrees of changes that happen. Once had a student simply faint at the masculine change," my teacher continues.

"I didn't faint," I hear my deeper voice reply.

"True," Professor Russo agrees. On my other side, the tutor holds my other arm.

"Am I okay? Am I hurt?" I can feel my heart racing. I can feel my body fighting the dampener, making my arm and wrist feel as if they're on fire.

"Stay here; take deep breaths," Professor Russo orders. Next to me, Tutor Lubit is doing as ordered, looking at me intently, helping me sync my breathing. "We'll explain it in the clinic," the professor assures me.

"Blake?" I turn to see Seb looking at me, not with those same wide eyes, but in deep concern as I'm led from the room.

"Let's give you a full physical first," Doctor Lim Falk says once we're in the school's clinic.

I'm out of the torn uniform and sitting on the examination table in loose pants and a shirt. My uncle is in the room, leaning back against the wall opposite me. I have this suspicion that if I stood up, I'd be nearly as tall as he is. He looks worried, one hand cupping his chin and the other arm around his waist.

"First, we'll do blood work, so you'll feel a bit of a prick on your finger, thank you," the doctor says as she walks me through each aspect of the exam.

When she gets to the expanded equipment, I hold up a hand. "Uncle Delmar, I need privacy for this part."

He looks back at me, then sighs and looks to the doctor, who asks me, "Are you sure, Blake? This will be uncomfortable, a bit scary even. Having a man in the room might be reassuring."

"You went through *True You*, right?" I ask her, and she nods. "So, you remember what the differences are like."

"It's been a while, Blake, and I didn't get a full physical. It just isn't something we do unless there is a problem."

"So, there is a problem," my uncle repeats and takes a few steps closer to me. He looks a bit shorter and a touch smaller than I remember, probably from his worried stance, slightly bent toward us, his head tilted to watch closely.

"So far there are no signs of physical harm, but Blake dimension shifted without any guidance. A talent manifesting suddenly is always cause for caution," the doctor explains.

"Dimensions?" I ask, and I note that my Uncle has taken another step toward me. "I thought maybe I'd moved across time."

The doctor tilts her head and considers for a moment. "Could you see what was going on in the classroom?"

"No, just gray everywhere."

"Chronomancers step between time, but they view what is happening, has happened, or will happen. I'm sure your uncle has explained all the various forms of magic there are."

I look at my uncle with a frown while asking, "Why would he know anything about that? He and Grandmother always remind me that all of this was a long time ago for them."

Doctor Falk blinks at me, then at my uncle. "Oh, perhaps you were waiting for Blake to learn everything in school?"

Her words sound like an accusation, making my uncle fold his arms over his chest and plant his feet in a wide stance; he doesn't look as big as he should. "We want Blake to learn with their … his peers unless he has questions."

I frown and snort in disbelief. My questions are almost always ignored when it comes to his work, my parents' work, or specifics about magic. Clothing attunements or minor medicinal spells are exceptions. "Can we just get this over with?" I complain.

My uncle steps out of the room, and the doctor instructs me to remove my trousers. I breathe in and out, as I always do for these types of exams, and discover that the invasiveness is different—not really better or worse. What's annoying is how much more reactive these male body parts are to every type of interaction. But just as the doctor ignores the changes, I try to do likewise. When that doesn't work, I run through boring lists again.

"Let's talk about what you were feeling at the moment right before you dimension shifted," Counselor Milford says once I'm seated in her office. She met with my grandmother and uncle first, while I ate lunch with Doctor Falk. Now it's my turn in the chair across from her. *Best to try to take this seriously and get it over with.*

I consider the question, then shrug. "I felt like everyone was looking at me. Half the class had changed, but everyone was staring at *me*."

"And that made you feel?"

"Annoyed, worried, scared, I guess." The band around my wrist burns again.

"Every time you try to travel to a different dimension, that will prevent it, so it will hurt," the psychologist points out.

"I wasn't trying to do any magic."

"Not consciously, but our talents often manifest unconsciously, and they can activate under stress. You have quite a talent, Blake."

I glower and sink down a bit in my chair, but it's harder to make myself small when I'm so much taller and wider. Doctor Falk said that my body is more like a young man of twenty or so, not a teenager. Apparently, the uniforms are designed to adapt to the normal range of changes based on the spells. The spells of *True You* are supposed to help us learn what it's like to be a teen, but because I'm a freak, it went wrong.

Those aren't things I want to talk about now, so I try to jump on the less personal subject she's offered. "I've never heard of dimension traveling before," I state, trying to make my voice higher pitched, but it only sounds worse.

"It is uncommon, but then you are uncommon in several ways." I sit up straight and stare at her. "Obviously both Doctor Falk and I have been aware of your intersex status from your enrollment." I feel a rush of anger through my body at this information. This was supposed to be my secret to share or not. "Sadly, your grandmother and uncle didn't sign the permission forms, so we weren't allowed to tell your professors and the rest of the staff."

"Why does anyone need to know? It'll all be fixed by the end of the term anyway," I growl out softly.

Counselor Milford furrows her brow slightly. "Is that what you think *True You 101* will do for you? That it will pick a sex, pick a gender, and then you'll be common? I hope it doesn't; I like you just as you are."

"You don't even know me; this is only the second time I've ever been in your office. And checking in with me the first week at Reinholdt is hardly getting to know me," I point out with a bit more passion than I'd planned.

"It's true that I haven't spoken with you face to face again, but I get copies of your journal entries when they mention mental and emotional issues."

I feel my mouth drop open, and I bend down over my knees and put my head in my hands. *She's seen everything I've written, then, since last year?* I recall the various topics I've written about in my journal and groan. "If you've read all of that, why would you think my continuing to be so abnormal would be a good thing?" I demand, looking up at her.

"I didn't use the words normal or abnormal—those aren't proper to use regarding gender or sexuality. I said uncommon and common. All of us have commonalities, and most of us have something uncommon as well that makes us unique. Your intersex nature is only one of those uncommon factors, but it is an important one."

I listen to the psychologist as she talks and shake my head. "That's easy for you to say, but you don't live it. You haven't been called a freak or a boy-girl or dozens of other things."

"That was back in the mortal realm. Has any of that happened to you since you entered Reinholdt?"

I shake my head. "I'm more careful now; I just don't let anyone know."

Counselor Milford sighs and holds out her hand. Once I take it, she squeezes mine and says, "That has to be one of the saddest things I've heard in weeks, Blake. I'm afraid you won't be able to keep that secret anymore."

I feel the lump in my throat move as I swallow. *See, I knew this was going to be the worst year of my life.*

I really want to jump into another dimension the moment my grandmother confirms I'm intersex as we sit facing Headmaster Tennison in his office. Of course, Grandmother doesn't stop with just confirming the reports from Doctor Falk and Counselor Milford. She has to add, "She was horribly bullied in mortal school; we were just trying to protect her. Him," Grandmother adjusts as she looks toward me.

"This information should have been shared with us here at Reinholdt," Headmaster Tennison says flatly to my grandmother, uncle, and myself.

"Why?" my uncle demands. He's leaning forward, glaring at the headmaster, who gives a slow blink, then motions with one finger in a circular pattern, casting a simple spell.

"Now no one can possibly overhear us, even if they're attempting to," Tennison states.

He leans forward and looks at each of us until he's staring directly at my uncle. "You do something foolish in your career, and you pay for it, your family pays for it. You keep information from us at the Institute, and you endanger other children. I won't allow that."

I'm a danger to the other students? I look at my uncle who has tilted his head up and is glaring back with more anger than I've ever seen from him before. They are acting like rivals, but how could my headmaster even know my uncle, who was in Europe until my parents' disappearance? *The enchanted realm isn't that small, is it?*

"I will not tolerate anyone harming my child—my sister's child," my uncle quickly amends. I catch my grandmother's worried glance at my uncle and how she puts a hand on his arm.

"No one would harm Blake," the headmaster states firmly. "We don't allow such things. However, given that we weren't told, we haven't prepared *True You 101* appropriately, and harm may come of it, not only for Blake but for Haydar Plank as well."

My uncle is shaking his head, and my grandmother has her hand up to her mouth, but the headmaster continues. "That course is vitally important to young mages, because it helps them sort out who they are on social levels that will impact how they are treated not only in the mortal world but also in ours. Each section is created to allow representatives of all the transmutable categories to be experienced, not merely so the final spell will align with their true selves, but so they can help each other though the changes. In terms of gender identity, we want a balance when we can achieve it, because that identity can be the most challenging, particularly if one is primarily living in the mortal realm. It's too far along in the course to change student pairings for this part of the class."

"I don't understand," I say. There are only twenty of us in this grade; there aren't any more students to add. The adults turn to look at me. "I can still help Haydar out when he tries female on; I've passed as that for, well, forever."

The headmaster leans back in his chair and steeples his fingers below his chin for a few seconds. "Blake, you were surprised by the degree of changes your body went through on the masculine side, correct?"

"Yes, sir," I say. I should have known it wouldn't be easy for me when my entire life has been nothing but confusion in terms of what people see and expect from me. Objectively—to use a word Counselor Milford used—what I looked like was more extreme compared to the other girls in my class because my body also became more mature. However, it was my reaction to the changes and my fear of being the center of attention that drew everyone's notice.

"Professor Russo and the doctors all tell me that your feminine transformation is likely to be as extreme for you, though now that we know, we can help you prepare. But Haydar won't have a buddy to help him figure it out as smoothly, because you'll also be dealing with changes at the same time. Do you understand now?" the headmaster asks.

I'm silent for a few moments, trying to figure out why it would be shocking to be more feminine. So, my breasts get bigger, and probably my hips, too. I suppose hormonal balance will be different. Then I glance down at my lap, and I know what he's talking about. "Oh, that," I say, my face aflame with embarrassment.

A look around confirms that my grandmother and uncle's eyes also went to my trousers, and they both look away when I catch their gaze.

"Yes, that," the headmaster repeats. "Before this spell, Counselor Milford says that you considered your body to be abnormal," he goes on, looking at the notes in my file.

I nod and look to the side, away from the adults.

"Where did you get the idea that you were … abnormal?"

I grimace, then turn to face him. "Are you kidding? Everywhere, everything, tells me that I'm not right. Grandmother told me that when I was born the nurses and doctors argued that I should be fixed. Then no one ever talked about it again with me. They could have just fixed me, but they didn't, and then it was this big horrible secret."

The headmaster's lips press into a thin line, and his gaze snaps to my grandmother as I continue. "Sex education in school—mortal school—showed me what's normal; I knew I didn't look like that. When I wanted to talk about it … I knew you were ashamed when you just said it would be all right or you didn't answer my questions directly," I point out to my guardians. My voice sounds so angry, so intense, that I flinch at the tone as I speak.

My uncle closes his eyes as my grandmother reaches for me and I pull my arm away. "I don't recall ever saying you were normal or not, because we're not ashamed of you, Blake," she tells me, but her voice sounds weak, and I know she doesn't really mean it.

"Blake," the headmaster says to get my attention, and I look at him. "I'm sure your family was merely trying to protect you."

"Of course we were," my uncle grinds out. "So much happened that we thought if we acted like everything was normal, maybe her—his—differences wouldn't be so important."

"But we made it worse—I'm so sorry, my dear," Grandmother says as she strokes my arm. I shake my head and pull farther away, causing Counselor Milford, who has been quietly observing from across the room, to come over to me.

"We're sorry," my uncle says after a few moments, and my grandmother nods. "What can we do to fix this?"

"I have a few suggestions," the headmaster begins. "Continued consultations with Counselor Milford, to begin with."

I sink down in my chair at that directive.

"Every day for the rest of the term, and then we'll see what's necessary," the psychologist explains. "I want to offer you all a family session one day a week as well—whatever will fit into your work schedule, Mr. Trudeau."

My uncle and grandmother exchange a look, then my uncle nods. "I have a tricky schedule, but I'll make time. Blake is the most important person in my life."

I shake my head but stay where I am, with Counselor Milford holding one of my hands.

"Good," the headmaster agrees. "Second, I've asked a couple juniors and seniors who are also intersex to mentor Blake through the rest of the term."

I blink and sit up straighter. *There are people like me right here in this school?* "There are others?" I ask.

"Yes," says Headmaster Tennison, "the rate of intersex children is less than two percent in the mortal world, but for mages it runs around five percent—more than double. There is a first year who is intersex as well, and I'll expect you to help them when they take *True You* next year. I think it's only fair, considering that others are going to be helping you."

"Yeah, yeah, I just didn't know," I reply. I relax in my seat, giving my grandmother access to caress my arm when I do so. I roll the new information around in my head. *I'm not alone. I'm not the Institute freak I thought I was.*

"The final suggestion will require Blake to be brave, but I think he can do that. Since the incident in the classroom has drawn the attention of the entire student body, we can use this as an opportunity to educate everyone," the headmaster explains.

"This will also be a chance for us to assess the course and see if we need to make any other adjustments," Counselor Milford adds.

"This isn't Professor Russo's fault," I begin, but both the doctor and the headmaster are shaking their heads.

"This is our fault," my uncle states. We lock eyes for a moment, then I look away. There is more being hidden from me, but right now I need to be brave, as the headmaster said.

Chapter 8: Not Alone, Not Abnormal

I can feel the magics pulling the air around me, tugging at every hair on my body—not the fiery pain from before—but still making me aware of what little control I have over this talent. The dampener on my wrist is keeping me in my place between Professor Russo and Counselor Milford. Over a hundred pairs of eyes are looking back at me from the chairs in the auditorium.

"I'm pleased that none of you seem outraged by this information," the headmaster ends his opening announcement. "Reinholdt needs to be a place of discovery and growth. We're going to use this opportunity to educate all of us—teachers, staff, and students—about the full spectrum of mage life that we have not done a proper job of addressing in the past."

The headmaster looks to my family and motions us to step forward. I shake my head, and Counselor Milford keeps her arm around me as my guardians approach the front of the stage.

"Mrs. Usha Trudeau and Mr. Delmar Trudeau are Blake's grandmother and uncle. They will now give you some background that I hope you will listen to with your hearts as well as your ears," the headmaster instructs. He steps back to allow my guardians to come up to the floating projection horn.

Grandmother says, "When Blake was born, the doctor told my daughter and her husband that they had either a baby boy or girl—they could decide. They were prepared for a healthy baby, a precocious one who might do something magical in a mortal hospital, but they weren't prepared for such a mundane issue."

Mundane? Not the word I would have chosen at all. I feel Counselor Milford's grip squeeze my shoulders for a second, and I relax a bit.

"We had wanted to have a home birth; it would have been simpler, but that would have meant risky travel. My daughter's health wasn't as strong as I'd hoped, and my own talents as a healer lie more in medications than directly healing the body, so we had no choice other than a nearby mortal hospital, given where we lived at the time. As I hope you've all learned, crossing between the mortal and enchanted worlds is dangerous for pregnant women and children under five. Even if we'd been near enough to a portal, it wouldn't have been a wise move." Grandmother takes a moment and dabs at her eyes. I put my hand on Counselor Milford's, and she squeezes it.

"The nurses, the doctor, they were very insistent that something was wrong with the baby; it was upsetting my daughter. I couldn't risk telling them that for our people this might be considered a blessing—as you know, the rules against revealing ourselves are strict. I should have risked it; I should have said more …" My grandmother trails off as my uncle puts an arm around her and pulls her toward him to kiss the side of her head. I feel my stomach sour, hearing about the stress my mother was put under just to bring me into the world.

The audience patiently remained attentive but quiet, as Grandmother continued. "When the doctors saw we weren't willing to make a choice and wouldn't simply sign their forms to let them choose, they let us go. We decided it was best to let Blake just be Blake. Other than a penis paired with a vagina, there was nothing unusual about her body. I suppose we shouldn't say 'her,' which isn't correct. Even though it was my daughter's wish that we not gender Blake, I'm afraid we haven't done the best job of it; especially after their deaths. I'm sorry, Blake," Grandmother says as she looks over at me.

I nod and run into her arms, pulling her small body to my huge one. My uncle puts a hand on my shoulder and squeezes it. He gives a strong smile and a nod when I look at him, my eyes a few centimeters higher than his.

The auditorium is oddly quiet, with only a few soft sounds. I look out as we free ourselves and see my *True You* classmates all seated together. Several of the new boys are dabbing at tears, but a couple of the others are palming their eyes to hide their emotional reactions. Haydar, Eva, and Seb are all just smiling grimly at me.

Not far from them is the theater club, with Victoria smiling at me and Wigheard nodding his head. He gives me a thumbs up for some reason. The rest of the club is just looking at me, with no extreme reactions. Efemena's boredom is probably a reflection of how mortal she finds this entire fuss.

Then the questions come, and the doctor, nurse, counselor, and Professor Russo all stand up to answer, explaining how common my condition is. I brace myself for rude questions or outright attacks, but none come.

Most responses deal with genetics and hormones, something I find interesting to learn for the first time, while other answers I already knew or guessed. They ask about the rarity of it, and then the two seniors, two juniors, and one first year stand up to show that I'm not alone. I feel my mouth drop open as Victoria and Wigheard stand up. Wigheard gives me a huge grin and a bow. No one in the rest of the audience seems surprised, simply curious. All four of the older intersex people walk up to stand in front of the stage, while the first year sits back down at a nod from the teacher near them.

"Due to the circumstances," the headmaster explains, "we are going to ask for a volunteer to be Blake's course partner for the remainder of *True You 101*. Because of this, Haydar Plank will need a new partner as well."

I turn my eyes up to look at Haydar, who is looking down, eyes narrowed, mouth set, but before he can rise to his feet, Seb's voice rings out, "Blake is my friend. I'm honored to help out. That hasn't changed," he says, looking right back at me.

"I was assigned her—his—I'm sorry, I'm not sure what to use now," Haydar stumbles as he stands up and speaks out. "I have no problem being Blake's course partner." The two boys exchange looks and then nod at each other.

Several more in the course also raise their hands or stand up. I sit up straight, feeling tears in my eyes. No one is running from me; no one is scared of me. I look over at Counselor Milford, who squeezes my hand. "That's my class," Professor Russo whispers with pride.

The headmaster turns to us with a shrug. "I think the choice is yours, Blake," he says, and his floating projection horn amplifies his words for the crowd. They all stop talking and look at me.

I look toward my grandmother and uncle. My uncle is wiping his eyes, but my grandmother is making a circular "get on with it" motion with her hand.

I get to my feet and step up next to the headmaster. "Thank you," I say into the narrow end of the horn and then laugh at how odd my voice sounds to me when it's so loud. "I think I should stay with Haydar, because every one of you already has a buddy. If the others like me are willing to help us—us both—I would be grateful. But …" I pause and look at everyone, stopping at Seb before I continue, "I want to help all of you in any way I can, and I hope you'll help me, too. Together, maybe we can all figure out who we are and become a stronger class."

The group is silent until Seb begins to clap, and they all follow suit. In a few minutes we're dismissed. I find myself surrounded by classmates I talk with all the time as well as ones I've never said a word to. Unlike all those mortal shows, no one belittles or insults me. No one even shoots me a dirty look.

Wigheard gently pushes through the crowd and puts an arm around me. In my current body I see and feel how he isn't quite as large as I thought he was. "We'll all be here if you need help, Blake, but as often happens, the adults are overreacting, and I think you're going to be just fine."

"I wish I had known; I'd been wanting someone I could talk to," I tell him—*them*.

"Now I'm hurt you think you couldn't talk to me before. I mean, I am all that, but still approachable," they tell me while striking a pose.

"You are definitely all that," I chuckle. When we stop laughing, I look down, then up again. "Do you prefer 'they,' or what?"

"The masculine pronouns are okay, unless you want to use some honorific, like 'Sir' or 'Lord,'" he jokes, then his face takes on the most serious expression I've seen when he isn't on stage. "Each of us is unique, Blake. When the course is done, tell us what you prefer. Yeah?" he asks with a wink that returns him to his normal persona.

"Yeah, I will," I reply, though I'm curious about that order.

Wigheard moves away, and other students come up to wish me well or give me a handshake or hug. I see the other intersex students have gathered into a small group—even the first year has joined them. I wonder why Victoria didn't come to me, but I pull my attention back to Brizo, who has tugged on my arm to get my attention.

"I thought you were lucky, right, getting this jacked up body instead of this mess," he says with a motion toward his acned face.

I hadn't thought about it that way. My current body is an adult's; I'm through all that puberty stuff already. Does that mean the horniness is just regular guy stuff? "Some things stay the same, teen or adult," I tell Brizo and a few of the other new boys around me. When they stare at me in confusion, I make a vague gesture downward. "This is out of control."

That gets a round of laughter from the group. Each new boy takes a moment to whisper about some weird thing that turned them on, making the course buddies standing nearby blush until the headmaster uses the speaker to remind us that classes will resume their schedule in ten minutes.

Seb lingers until most of the other students are gone, then holds out one hand. I take it and then pull him into a hug. He puts his arms around me and seems to relax everywhere except in one area that presses against my own groin. "Oh," I whisper to him as we separate.

"I didn't think I'd like girls in that way, but I liked you even after I figured that out—guess we know why now, huh?" he says softly. I don't mention that being solely interested in one sex is almost as rare as being intersex in the mage world, because we'll tackle that in class after the Solstice.

I think of how I've found some boys and some girls equally attractive myself, even before this change, and how I couldn't tell, given the fact that every emotion seems to play out in my groin right now. "I can relate," I tell him anyway, and he chuckles and steps back as Eva and Haydar join us before we can continue.

"We were thinking of hitting up a café for a hot chocolate or soda on the way to the rails after school lets out. Give our new bodies a test run as a team," Haydar suggests.

I glance around but don't see my family anywhere. "Great," I say.

"Good, because this is sort of freaking me out," Eva says in a nice baritone voice as he motions with one hand up and down his new body.

"It's your graaaaandmother," the goat head on my bedroom door announces a few minutes after I come inside and shut it. Neither she nor Uncle questioned why I didn't come home until after the sun was well down.

I sigh and run my too-large hands over my face a few times. I'm still in the borrowed clothing from school, though I have the newly attuned uniform in an extra backpack, also borrowed from school. My current body was strong enough to handle both bags fairly easily when I went with the others after school let out.

I look at both on my bed and decide not to move them before saying, "You may come in."

"Did you want some dinner, Blake?" Grandmother asks as the door opens, but she just stands in the doorway.

"We had some pastries and stuff after school," I say, then wince. I sound so harsh, even though I'm trying to be calm. "Sorry I didn't text or call."

"We thought you might have a meeting or something after the … events," she replies, glancing away.

I take a few steps toward her, but she doesn't move away or come inside. "Am I that scary right now?" I ask, trying to chuckle.

That gets her to take a few steps inside, and she puts her hands on my face. "You have a shadow forming. Your uncle will need to show you how to shave," she comments. She smiles up at me, then takes a deep breath.

"Please just say what you're thinking. I don't know that I can handle more … attempts to soften what you feel," I plead, grasping her hands in mine as she tries to turn back to the door.

"We talked after we came home. For a long time."

"You and Uncle Delmar?"

Grandmother moistens her lips, then nods. "Yes, about what happened today. About the past. The decisions we made—or didn't make—just *did*. It was all so different after the accident." I don't press her on that term but just gently offer her my desk chair. After I sit on the edge of my bed, standing and readjusting myself just once, she smiles and adds, "I miss her so much. I thought maybe … but you are you, Blake. I can't have my daughter back through you."

I blink in shock. That is not what I was expecting to hear, so I push just a touch. "Mum, you mean?"

"Yes—Hazel, your mother, my daughter. My only child. There were times you acted so much like her that sometimes I thought you could be her. I realized after everything at school, here talking with your uncle … I've been labeling you 'her,' but you may not be a 'her.'"

"But that's what I want," I counter.

Grandmother smiles sadly. "You haven't been a boy—no, a man—for a full day yet. Don't be so quick."

"Yeah, you haven't fully experienced the pros or cons," Uncle Delmar's voice draws our eyes to the open doorway.

"You're still here," I observe without moving from the bed, though I feel like I should stand up for some reason.

"I told work I needed to take the evening off."

"Because your niece is messed up and caused a scene."

"No, no," he says as he comes right inside. He motions toward the door, and one of the dining room chairs comes floating in as he talks. "Because you are the single most important part of my life. You are literally the only reason I'm here at all, Blake." He sits down on the chair, and we are all silent for a moment.

"You need to teach him to shave," Grandmother orders, making us huff out a laugh.

"No point in doing it now when it will just keep growing overnight," Uncle points out.

"Tomorrow morning?" I ask hopefully.

"Yeah, tomorrow morning, before breakfast, I'll come here with my razors to help you figure it all out."

"Isn't there a spell to just get it done?"

"To stop the growth, sure, but even that's tricky."

"Messing with the balances in the body is challenging; most men just shave," Grandmother offers.

"Cool," I agree with the plan. It isn't as cool as I hoped by the time I've managed to give myself several lightly bleeding nicks before I finish dressing the next morning.

The four older students are sitting on the benches along one of the walls in the *True You* classroom. I know Wigheard and Victoria, but not really the other two. I've seen them both around, but I've never talked to either of them. I have heard rumors about them both, nothing to do with their gender.

Nima McDonald's family primarily lives in the enchanted realm and she's—is that still correct?—best friends with Efemena. Nima can't be intersex; she's such a she in every way. Her long light-brown hair is always done up in a fashionable style that I can't imagine achieving without using magic. Today's is a corkscrew-like structure rising a good foot above her head with cascading bangs falling in a V-shape framing her face. Her skin is quite pale and looks almost poreless, though I see now there is a sheen about it that suggests makeup. Her almost copper eyes are outlined in black with a scroll pattern at the outer edges, and her lips are a deep crimson. In the mortal world we'd call her style Lolita Goth, which she's sort of achieving by adding on a few cute greyscale ribbons and pins to her uniform and sticking to the fuller knee-length skirt option.

Nima gives me a glance up and down, then a simple nod before looking at a tablet she was using when I walked into the classroom. Being fine with my body parts doesn't mean being friendly or chatty, I guess.

The same unfriendliness is true for Su-Bin Kennard, whom I only know because the entire school only has around a hundred students. As far as I know he or she—I'm not sure as I look for telltale gender cues—just continues to poke around on a smartphone. I settle on a generic pronoun in my head as I try to puzzle Su-Bin out. They are wearing the school uniform loosely with the knee-length shorts but generic top and blazer. Their black hair is a buzz cut, but the face is not particularly masculine or feminine, just a rather generic human shape. I can't see any makeup, but the fingers working the phone are more feminine. I know they work in the school kitchens, and I've heard they take culinary classes on the side from some mortal school, but that's pretty much it. For a senior, Su-Bin keeps a low profile.

Only Wigheard and Victoria look at me as Eva and I walk past them. Seb is already at his seat, but Haydar is right behind us. The guys have been very helpful since yesterday, answering text messages at a moment's notice. Who knew just taking a shower could raise questions?

We all drop off our journals, and then class begins with introductions of the visitors. "We have four upper-class students joining us for the next few weeks," Professor Russo says before saying each one's name and waiting for them to stand up.

"While these students have agreed to help a few of you specifically, they wanted me to tell you that they are happy to answer any questions you might have one-on-one during class or outside of it. Su-Bin requests that you understand that they get very busy in the hour before lunch and for the hour after it, and that they have a job that takes up several of their evening and weekend hours, but they will get back to you if you message them. You should all have the contact numbers for our new assistants on your Institute list."

I smile at the four of them, getting a nod from each before they sit back down. Only Wigheard looks interested in the class after this point whenever I glance at them during our small group exercises and general class discussions.

At the end of class, our foursome gathers to walk out. "This still feels weird," Eva confesses as he shakes one leg, then the other. "Is it bothering you as much?" he casually asks me when Haydar and Seb just roll their eyes.

"I'm not sure I'd say bother so much as I feel like my balance is off," I reply.

"Oh, that's true; our center of gravity is different from a girl's," Haydar says with a slight frown.

"At least we won't have to go through that time of the month, right?" Seb says the final word a bit louder, and Tutor Lubit shakes his head. If Seb really believes that, I have to wonder whether he's even read the chapter.

"Looks like you're all getting along," Wigheard interrupts us softly. "They're fine; they know how to contact us," he says more loudly to Su-Bin and Nima, who have been waiting. *Where did Victoria go?*

As we leave class, Eva squeezes my hand once before letting Wigheard take hold of my arm and lead me to theater club. "How are you really doing, Blake?" he whispers.

"I'm not sure yet. This is very different."

"Yes, the female body will also be very different," he tells me. I'm shocked into silence for a few minutes as we walk into the drama club room.

"But I, you know," I whisper when we take seats, "have my period and everything."

"Oh, wow, it isn't all about that," Wigheard replies with a snort, but the rest of the incoming students ignore it. "Not that I know exactly what will happen to you. I never had a period before and don't have it now, but when I became female it was quite overwhelming until Su-Bin and Nima took the time to help me process it all."

I bite my lip and look around but don't see her, so I lean into Wigheard to inquire, "Is Victoria keeping her—*their*—intersex a secret? Normally we chat, but now …"

"Victoria will have to speak for herself. Feminine pronouns are her preference, by the way. Mine are masculine, Nima's are feminine, Su-Bin prefers the old-fashioned 'they' forms," Wigheard informs me.

Other than Wigheard, I had just assumed all their pronouns without asking, which was super rude of me. That triggers another thought. "Are you and the others all still …" I make a vague hand gesture toward myself.

"Intersex? It isn't a bad word, Blake. I think the textbook still says 'hermaphrodite,' which isn't quite correct," Wigheard comments and rolls his eyes.

That's right—that is the term the book uses, along with something called "gynandromorph," which is even more complicated and a lot rarer—well, everywhere, based on the further reading I did last night. I realized that the reason I didn't see myself in the chapter or the textbook before was because of the terms I was looking for. "Yeah, intersex," I repeat. I want to lean forward to indicate he should continue, but Haydar and Seb told Eva and me last night that moving toward someone is like challenging them or asking for intimacy, so I've been monitoring what I do with my body, fighting to keep still and "guy distant," as Seb said.

"I still have pieces of both sets of external organs; inside it doesn't function, so no monthly cycle for me, but also no, you know," Wigheard adds in a whisper.

The entire club is now present; Victoria gives me a sad smile when I notice her. Everyone chats until Professor Hermans starts our meeting. I try to focus on what the others are saying until our director asks for clarification on a design I made for the upcoming show. "This is more stage craft than costumes," she points out.

I look at the sashes I've sketched out for our host to wear to introduce each segment. "I guess, but they wear them," I point out.

"I love the idea of title cards, but they do need to be big enough for the audience to read—how about you collaborate with sets for this one show?" she commands rather than asking, so I exchange looks with that department and everyone nods.

After the meeting, and for every day that week, Victoria seems to be slipping out of rooms or taking a later train or bus whenever I want to talk to her. Maybe next week will flow more easily when I look more like her.

"Now I am jealous," Seb says, her voice higher as she looks down at her new chest, then over at mine. I want to put my arms over my chest to give my glare extra punch, but it doesn't work with the extra padding I now have. I'm actually pleased, but I don't want to say that out loud to anyone.

"None of that," Eva says sternly. She's helping Haydar adjust her jacket over her own new breasts, but she's still paying attention to us. Nima is standing nearby and swats Seb's arm for emphasis.

"Ouch! I can't make jokes as a girl?" Seb demands.

"Make them about yourself all you like but know that's a short road to self-loathing for you mortal-worlders," Nima tells him. "No decent woman attacks another woman for her body. I think you folks call it body-shaming. That won't fly here, so save it for out there."

I try to ignore my ample chest and move my hips a bit to feel that change. Whoa, I can rotate my hips a lot more with a lot less effort, it seems. But it also feels off—too loose, too something that I don't want to admit.

I swallow and shake my head when Nima touches my shoulder and asks, "You need to talk?" Yeah, I'm not talking to her about how Headmaster Tennison was correct about missing my penis. Small as it was, it was still very much there. "Maybe, but not here," I emphasize by glancing around with my eyes.

"You can text me. My phone will pick up, even across the portal," Nima reminds me. I appreciate her attention, but I really wish Victoria were here. She barely speaks to me at drama club now.

"Do we sound that much different?" Haydar asks, pulling me out of my thought. She's wincing at the sound of her voice.

"Not too much, but then I get the feeling that you guys were a bit behind the puberty timeline," Eva says, lowering her voice on the last two words.

"No slap for that?" Seb hisses. "That was totally taunting and body shaming."

"I was trying to be honest and diplomatic. That's gonna be a hard one for you," Eva says pointedly at Seb.

"Seb is learning to tone it down, right?" I counter with another pointed look at him.

"Unless hormones really change things, I'm planning to still be me," he replies.

All four of us look at Nima now, who blinks, then sighs. "Read the textbook much? Personalities won't automatically change, just like when you were all male. But as you get feedback from others, it may change a bit to help you fit into the gender others are going to assume you have."

I feel my eyes go a bit wider at the reminder that gender and biology are not the same thing, even if they seem so tightly connected back in the mortal realm. I put my arm around Haydar as she steps closer to me. "We're in this together, girls," I say softly.

Eva nods with a grin, while Nima rolls her eyes. No one told her to identify as more feminine, so I don't feel sorry for her that she's stuck helping us more than Wigheard or Su-Bin or Victoria. Why isn't Victoria here? I thought the older students had agreed to help us, but other than that first day, she's been absent without explanation.

"Everyone back to their seats; let's have some starting questions," Professor Russo orders. Next to her, Tutor Lubit is looking lovely with her new body and not a bit awkward as she starts reading through the first image projected in front of us all.

Dear Journal,

Mortals suck.

For the full six days I was a guy, the biggest problems I had were wet dreams, adjusting to the feeling of my body in gym class, and realizing just how many boys and girls I actually find hot at school. No wonder Seb has been a jerk this term with all these out of control reactions.

Outside of school, depending on the neighborhood I was moving through, I could do whatever I wanted. Yeah, there were the few sneaky looks that I bet were because of my skin color, but I was so large, no one did anything. It probably helped that I was with friends or my uncle.

After a day as our original selves, three of us became full girls. Honestly, that felt more familiar to me. It wasn't like I was hung before, so contrary to Tennison's worries, I don't feel like I was missing much. The higher voice was a bit unnerving, I'll admit, but I really felt pretty good.

That very first afternoon, some dicks on the subway decided to harass us. I mean, sure, Seb is a cute girl, and Haydar's okay in a geeky way, but seriously some of that was rapey. I'd never heard such things before.

Like an avenging angel, Victoria showed up and offered to curse them for us. I was so surprised, happy, confused—everything—to see her that I couldn't say anything. Eva just grabbed Seb's hand, and we all followed them toward our homes.

"I need some advice," I blurt out to my grandmother when I find her relaxing in the living room the next afternoon. My uncle is nowhere to be seen, but he's been heading to work a few hours early the past few days because of some revelations or something that have drawn the mortal realm's attention toward us. He's working at the various publications to keep their speculations in check and probably to fix any inconvenient facts, but I know enough to not try to learn more.

Grandmother looks up from the book she was reading and smiles at me. "Oh, wow, look at you!" she says, then puts one hand over her mouth. "Blake, I didn't mean to say that this is better, or worse for that matter, than the way you were yesterday or last week or before that …"

"How do you ask a friend why they're ignoring you without risking losing their friendship?" I rush ahead to stop the awkward second-guessing my family has been doing ever since the headmaster called them to task about keeping my intersex nature a secret.

Grandmother sits up and puts her book on the stand next to her chair as I take a seat adjacent to her on the sofa. "If they are your friend, I think they would welcome the question, though you might want to consider how to word it."

"What do you mean?"

"Instead of asking, 'why are you ignoring me,' maybe ask them if there is a problem, because you haven't talked with them for a few days. Give them a chance to realize they've hurt your feelings without making them feel attacked. Do you see the difference?"

"Yeah, yeah, I think so."

"With my patients, mortal or mage, I have to do a similar thing for some of them. If I just ask why they've put on twenty pounds in the last year, they get defensive, but if I ask them if they've been feeling stressed, they might talk about eating, too."

I nod a few times. While my family has been vague about my parents and didn't want to talk about my body for fear of making me feel weird, they have always been pretty good with questions about other stuff. Counselor Milford advised me to just ask about everyday matters to help them ease into the idea of being more honest with me, so I've been trying to do that the past few days.

"Do you want to tell me more?" Grandmother asks.

"No, no, not now. Do you need help with dinner?"

"It will be just you and I again tonight, so I was hoping you'd help me eat some leftovers."

"Sure! I love leftovers," I reply with a grin.

"Come to the dinner table, then, at the regular time. I'm going to try and read a few more chapters," Grandmother tells me as she picks up her book again.

I stand up and head back to my room to do some homework.

My mind can't concentrate for long, and soon I'm looking at my phone, finger hovering over Victoria's number. I bite my lip, then press.

I hold the phone up to my ear and wait for the rings, about to give up, when I hear her ask, "Blake? What's wrong?"

"Victoria, could we … hang out and talk, if you have time? I've missed seeing you, talking with you." I bite my lip again.

A few silent moments pass, then she says, "I can be there in a few, if you have time now."

"Yes, great, that would be great," I reply. I'm babbling like an idiot, so I press my lips together to stop speaking.

"Good, good. See you soon."

I listen to the connection die, then stare at my phone. My heart is pounding loudly in my whole head. My family knows the Hileses, but normally they see me with Seb or talking about Seb. Without another thought, I walk out of my room, snag my keys on the way, and call out, "I'm meeting a friend outside, but I'll be back soon, Grandma!" I don't even wait for her answer.

I sit on the porch in the swing that was there when we moved in. I'm hardly moving as I look the direction that Victoria should come from. I force myself to stay seated when I see her, waving when she does. I don't stand up at all when she comes onto the porch and sits on the other side of the swing.

We're quiet for a few minutes, then both try to speak at the same time. After some nervous laughter, I say, "You first."

Victoria pushes back a strand of her hair as she sighs. "I'm sorry I've been distant, Blake. I'm sorry I didn't figure out what was going on with you."

I feel my mouth fall open, so I close it and shake my head. "What? Why would you? That isn't something I expected."

"No, but I expect to be better aware of my friends. I mean, I know you and my brother are closer because of your ages, but since you joined drama, and then your questions about his behavior … I thought maybe we'd become closer. Though I've not done what I should've to really be much of a friend."

"What are you talking about? You've been a great friend up until our similarities were revealed." We are both silent again for several moments. "I thought you were embarrassed to know me."

Victoria gives me one of her pointed looks that generally gets everyone to behave as she wants, but that fades as she closes her eyes for a second. "I am embarrassed, but by me. I feel like I should have known something was going on with you since I've been through it too. But I just thought you were going gaga over my brother."

"I have no idea how I feel about your brother. Half the time I want to beat him, and the other half I just want to hang out and play and talk like we used to," I say.

"Oh, so your interest is like siblings, then," Victoria jokes.

I smile but shake my head. "Not quite. The thing is, I worked really hard to make everyone think I was a normal girl. I know that we're not supposed to say that, but that's how I felt." Victoria leans toward me but doesn't say anything, so I continue. "I told Seb that we moved from London for my uncle's job, but really it was because some girls at a previous school saw me in the gym locker room and started telling everyone about it. It got nasty."

I hadn't realized that my gaze had lowered during the confession until Victoria's hand on mine makes me look up. "Damn. That's just … I'm sorry that happened. It was never a secret for me or my family, but it wasn't casual conversation either. The person who helped me through *True You* is now in college, and we keep in touch. They found me that first week of classes—they just knew, or the administration told them, I'm not sure. I got a letter from the school when Paddy Gentletouch enrolled this year. I figured that there were no intersexed students last year."

"I thought we weren't supposed to talk to the younger kids about the course."

"We don't talk about the course, but we just let them know that we're also at school in case they have any concerns or problems and feel uncomfortable asking anyone else. Puberty doesn't quite work the same way for us, as you know."

I nod, but before I can ask a question, Victoria apologizes again. "You are forgiven," I simply say, parroting what Counselor Milford suggested I do when my uncle and grandmother were driving me crazy those first couple of days after everything came out at school.

Victoria smiles and relaxes then. "Good, good, because it's been killing me to make up excuses to not help you, see you, or talk to you."

We both smile and talk for a while about how these two days have been going. "I'm telling you a curse of hairy palms does wonders for that sort of talk," Victoria repeats as we both stand up after her phone alarm sounds.

"I don't think that's allowed outside of school," I reply with my best mimic of Eva's tone from a couple of weeks ago.

I walk her to the sidewalk, and then Victoria pauses for a second before turning back to me. "Blake, the others have told me that you haven't asked a lot of questions, but I know you must have some. Now that we've both admitted our embarrassments, I need you to know that you can ask me anything. I'll be blunt; that's me, but I'll be truthful."

I know exactly what to ask her.

Dear Journal,

I managed to eat leftovers with Grandmother when I came back inside from seeing Victoria. I'm glad I followed Grandma's advice, and that Victoria and I are talking again. I've been working on homework, or trying to work on it, for a couple of hours. We're supposed to write about what's going on with us every evening or morning, so that's what I'm struggling to do.

I think it's weird that the attunement spell Grandmother taught me has adjusted to this sex change, but the school uniform didn't. I get the general-vs.-specific aspect of the magic, but still, doesn't that seem odd?

I didn't know that people were still being attacked for being suspected of witchcraft into the twenty-first century in some parts of the mortal realm. This history class is almost as scary as last year's two-term one. I thought I'd be taking another history course in the next term after the Solstice, but I need to do some deeper work on what appears to be my talent, since I'm still wearing this damned bracelet to keep me from slipping out of dimensions. I wonder if that means I won't have to take Your Talents next year?

I asked Victoria if there were other intersex students who had fully transformed at the end of their second year. She told me that she didn't know of any from her class. She didn't think anyone from the senior class changed that much either.

That's not what I wanted her to say.

I feel my body reshape itself from female back to me. I pause in my cataloging of changes and smile. That might be the first time in my life that I didn't attach "abnormal" as a descriptor to myself.

I look over at the quad of other intersex students and give them a grin. Wigheard grins back, while Nima just gives me a weak thumbs-up sign. Su-Bin actually smiles before looking up at the ceiling.

"Now that you all are back in your pre-term form, let's break into our discussion groups," Professor Russo orders.

I turn my desk slightly so I'm facing the other three students in our set. The others are girls, but instead of flashing back to bullying fears as I have before, I just return their shy smiles.

"Tutor Lubit is coming around with the discussion form. You know the routine by now. However, our guest students are available to join any group who would be interested. To help you decide if you'd like an additional viewpoint, know that today's grouping will be the one you have the entire second term of this course."

I pause, looking at the three girls—Brizo, Adella, and Porcia, whom we've teamed with for these discussions in the past—and they just shrug, but no one raises a hand. I look around and see several hands up already, so I just keep mine on my desk. As Wigheard passes by to join another team, he winks at me, and I smile back. The other intersex students go to other groups, and I'm grateful that we aren't being singled out this way. Then I pause at a new thought: *Am I supposed to represent all intersex people now for this discussion?*

"You okay, Blake?" Brizo asks me. I blush, worried that the other two are now looking at me, but they're reading through the form together as seatmates.

"We just talk about our own experiences, right?"

"Yeah, like always, though I think we can talk about what our study buddy said and did."

Adella and Porcia voice their agreement. Then Adella, whose turn it is to be group chair, takes the sheet and reads out the first topic. She asks, "What was the most surprising thing about female week for you personally?"

I expect the other three to look at me, but instead Porcia speaks up. "Given how much information we've had about female bodies, hormones, that sort of thing, I was amazed at how little my buddy seemed to know."

"Know or understand?" Brizo asks.

Porcia paused to think, then said, "I guess understand. He seemed surprised by everything that was happening. Not just for the first couple of hours, but the entire week. I don't think I've gotten so many text messages from one person in my life."

We each smile, but we've learned not to laugh during these group discussions, because the tutor is always lurking about, ready to remind us that this is not a place for teasing. I open my mouth before I can overthink my words. "It doesn't match the descriptions—not very well. Remember what it felt like when you became male? Even after a full day, walking was still odd."

"That's true," Adella agrees. "And the smell … that was probably different too."

Now they all do look at me, but they do so in a careful manner, not challenging but curious. "Yeah, males and females do have different smells, and tones of voice, and that center of gravity thing could be an issue running in the rain," I offer honestly, but with a touch of humor.

The other three smile but don't push me for me more information. Then Adella rereads the first topic before the tutor can come around to get us focused, embarrassing us in front of the entire class.

"I was worried about coaching my partner through a period, you know?" Porcia admits. She casually does a complicated trick with her pen, her swarthy, strong-looking fingers managing it easily. I know so little about her except that she portals to and from campus every morning and isn't part of any extracurricular activities. She stops twirling the pen after we all just stare in fascination for a few minutes.

Adella shakes her head, the brown braids down her back moving slightly. I know so little about her, too, except that she's taking at least one extra course this year, maybe because her parents are academics. That's what I've heard from others at least. "Did anyone have to help out with a period?" When no one admits it, she wonders out loud, "Did you have your period? I didn't, so maybe that's connected?"

"That would make sense," Brizo suggests. "I mean, if you both went through it, it would be easier to talk about it, share supplies, that sort of thing."

I can almost feel Eva's eyes staring at me, reminding me that my silence is basically lying. But it would be too embarrassing to admit that I was scared the second day when I thought I might be bleeding to death. Adella is also hesitant to share a lot about herself, so she doesn't push us all to talk more.

The discussion form is passed to Porcia. "What was the most surprising thing about male week for you personally?"

"We sort of mentioned that, right?" Brizo points out.

"Not really. We got sidetracked," Porcia counters.

We all look at each other, at our desks, then let our eyes slide in other directions. I can feel my heart pounding, but I can see Lubit glancing in our direction, so I take a breath and say softly, "Is sex all they think about?"

The others blush, then giggle and lean over the desks to be closer. "Thank the goddess! I thought I was just super perverted," Brizo chuckles.

"It isn't perverted, it's just, you know—nature," Porcia offers. The other two suck in their breath, and all three look at me with wide eyes. "I didn't mean," Porcia begins, but I just shake my head.

"No, it was quite horny for me. I was an adult, so I'm thinking it was worse for you all," I point out.

"That's right!" Brizo states a bit too loud, and Lubit glares at our group. A few other groups start laughing. All four of us sink down into our seats until the other discussion teams quiet down to murmur level again.

I'm going to be so glad when the Solstice gets here.

Chapter 9: This is Not a Costume

After the break, I'm surprised to see Seb standing and waiting for me at our old cafeteria two-person table spot. *Am I really?* Since four of us teamed up for the sex switches, he's been more like his old self. We saw each other at several Solstice gatherings, but his family was away most of the break. I can see the jocks toss him a few looks before they go back to isolating themselves with chatter and lunch.

I look at Victoria, who is in line behind me waiting to have her lunch rung up and motions with her head toward her brother. "Go on and try to salvage that friendship. He may have grown up a bit these past few weeks," she tells me. We haven't talked about much other than food while we've been in line because we've been texting or phoning regularly since our porch talk, so I don't take her suggestion as anything other than a hope that I can rekindle the older friendship.

I nod, then walk over and take my old seat, and Seb sits down. We talk about several things, then he leans over his tray and says, "I think I might not be gay."

I wipe my mouth, mulling that statement in my head a few times before answering. *Is that part of what's been going on with him?* There are lots of statistics I could spout off, but I channel our discussion group rules from *True You* instead and ask, "Why do you think that?"

Seb sighs and runs a hand over the back of his neck and up along his head, messing up his hair. "So, I guess I never explained why I thought I was gay, huh?"

I shake my head and move a bit closer to him. He's nervous and making his voice soft, so he must be ashamed or worried others might hear. "We can finish quickly and head outside," I remind him. He nods, and we do so.

The weather is lovely, but I'm mostly focused on my former and possibly reclaimed best friend, who is pacing a few times while I sit on top of one of the outdoor picnic tables. I smile gently when he stops.

He takes a deep breath, then sits down so he can look up at me. "They say that you just know if you're straight or gay." I know the "they" he means is the mass media and culture of the mortal realm, where we've both been living our entire lives. "But they never describe what it means to know that. I figured, because I found some boys attractive and frankly not any girls, I was gay. I've been trying to find all guys attractive, and I don't."

I want to interrupt and point out that finding everyone in any group attractive probably isn't how sexual orientation works, but I just nod at him encouragingly.

"But you … I realized over summer vacation that my missing you was, you know, sexy missing, too."

Now I feel a blush heat up my cheeks, but I just nod again.

"Then I noticed that I did find a couple of the girls attractive, and they were all taller, but not so feminine shaped—same as you are." When I make a face, he quickly adds, "And the guys I liked weren't the really big ones—even though I was trying so hard to like them and look like them—but the smaller guys who were into different things. I'm not explaining this very well," he whined and started to stand up.

I put my hand on his arm and said, "Our textbook said that just as with the greater variety of sexual types among mages, like more intersex people …" I motion toward my own chest. "… we also have a wider range of sexual orientations."

"But bisexual—is that the right word? I mean … do you know what you are, Blake?"

I blink at him and sit up straighter. All term long my sexual orientation hasn't been my focus at all. I start revealing my train of thought. "I just honestly don't find very many people attractive like that. I never thought to put a word on it before. Do we really have to? That isn't part of the final evaluations, I don't think."

"True," Seb agrees and leans against the table. "But is that just because the expectation is that we'll all reproduce, but we'll also have more relationships than mortals do?"

I raise my hands to make an exaggerated shrug. "I think these are questions for Russo and Lubit. I'm more worried about all this trying on different bodies the next few months."

"I'm anxious to get it over with, too," Seb admits. Then he puts one hand over mine. "If I have sexual feelings for you, does it piss you off? Scare you?"

"We're sixteen; I think it probably is supposed to scare us." I chuckle, but his gaze makes me take the question seriously. "I feel more relieved." Seb keeps looking at me, so I sigh and admit, "I think I've been having feelings about you for a while now. That's why the way you've behaved all first term has been so painful."

Seb looks down, then he lifts our hands and kisses the back of mine. "I don't know much about intersex people, but I'd like to learn more, if you can be patient."

"What if I'm not at the end of this? What if I look entirely different?"

"What if I am?" Seb counters.

I just sit there and shake my head. "When did you go from jock-wannabe-jerk to wisdom guru?"

"Let's say I'm learning."

I smile and copy his motion of bringing up our hands, kissing the back of his. "We can learn together, right?"

"Right," he agrees.

Dear Journal,

I know we're supposed to be supportive of each other in that course, but I had to really fight not to laugh out loud when Seb asked all his questions today about why mages can't be gay in class. I thought that was pretty clear in our textbook: We can be any type of sexual orientation, gender, race, sex, interspecies, or whatever. But the names mortals give to many of those categories don't reflect our realities.

Let me just quote the professor from my notes: "Concepts of strict personal categories are a reflection of the limited lives of mortals. All of you have grown up and lived in a mostly mortal world. These ideas you've learned could be harmful to yourself, your classmates, and your future in the enchanted world. Part of the process this term is to figure out what form is best suited to help you with your role in our world."

This raised the idea of the Fates again. Haydar and I talked about that on the block walk today, because Seb, for all the admissions of attraction between us, is still struggling with talking to me about these ideas he has about what he should be.

I know that makes me a total hypocrite because of my focus on becoming a girl. Isn't that different?

Crap.

Maybe it isn't different. I'm looking at this teenage boy's hand I currently have. It feels so off, but it's writing well, and it worked simply fine in classes or eating. I don't feel like me, but I don't feel horrible about this either. The fact that I could wear one of the uniform skirts tomorrow to school and no one would care isn't helping me reconcile this. Maybe that's just mortal culture's influence.

This should be fixed by now!

"Uncle Delmar?" my voice squeaks with the tell-tale signs of a boy just going through puberty. I am not enjoying this adjusted spell that has me becoming a teenager, as opposed to the adult form my first sex change triggered. My uncle looks up from his shoes, which he was putting on in his bedroom. He blinks in surprise because I don't normally come into his private space like this.

"Hey, Blake, what's going on?" He welcomes me in with a smile but doesn't stand up as he finishes his task.

"Is Grandma angry at me?"

That makes him pause again, but this time he also winces before putting on another smile as he sits up straight. "That's an odd question to ask. Your grandmother is pretty good about letting us know when she's angry or not to be messed with."

"Yeah, but what if the anger wasn't at what I did but what I was?" I'm staring at the floor and my uncle's feet. He doesn't say anything or move, so I'm forced to explain. "So this is the third week that I've been a boy, and each week she asks me to help her less and less with her medication prep or in the kitchen … she isn't talking with me as much."

My uncle's feet shift, and I look up as he stands and takes a couple steps toward me. I have to tilt my head back a bit more in this body. Uncle sighs, then puts his hands on my shoulders and looks me in the eye. "Hazel is—was—your grandmother's only daughter. You know that's so important for our people. While it wasn't fair of her to gender you all these years, she can know that in her head but not her heart. It isn't personal. Can you understand that?"

"Will she love me if I turn into a boy?" I counter. I can understand Grandmother's feelings—they mirror my own, but I'm also trying to be realistic with what might happen.

"As long as you're Blake, she's gonna love you. She'll just be really picky when you date girls—instead of being super picky when you date boys."

That brings a smile to my face as my stomach and chest unclench. "Basically, she's going to be picky if I date a different sex or gender?"

"Nah, that's my stupid mouth acting up. She's gonna be picky no matter who you date, trust me on this." My uncle cuts off any follow-up questions I might have but rolls his eyes at what must be his memories of dating … if he ever did that. I'll leave it for now.

I can figure out what's going on with the two of them once I'm all figured out. It's only a couple more months and balancing all these changes along with my classwork is proving to be a challenge.

"I thought we'd be switching bodies more often than this," Seb complains one afternoon when all four of us are trudging toward his and Eva's turn to go down their street.

For the past month, we've each been guys. Different sizes and shapes, different combinations of hair, skin, eyes, etc., but we've all been male—if we've been honest with each other. The other three in my class discussion group have been going back and forth between female and male. "I'm kind of getting used to the extra privileges," Eva tosses out as she runs a hand through the short blond haircut her current body is sporting.

"Privileges?" Seb repeats. "Mages are matrilineal."

"I think she means out here in Brooklyn, in the mortal realm," Haydar corrects him. Haydar's glasses have been tinted all day since the spell this morning, but his words feel like they're heavy for some reason. I know that Seb is unhappy that Haydar's body has been towering over his, but I also know that it isn't making Haydar pleased or comfortable either.

"Maybe this is us getting through the forms we won't have," Eva offers when we pause at the corner where we split up.

Haydar and Seb both get paler at the idea, so I take their speechlessness as an opportunity to pull Seb toward me. In a way, we've been dating since our lunchtime confession, or maybe we're just using this time to figure out what we're feeling. "This new form still make you horny?" I tease him.

Seb eyes me, taking in this week's form. Currently I'm still black, and a boy, but this time I'm shorter and definitely wider than I was last week. He shakes his head no. "I think it's the proportions, maybe. You're like a linebacker now."

"Nice!" I give him a little push with one hand, and he steps back, acting like I've really pushed him hard. Currently he has a swimmer's body, as Brizo would classify it, complete with a rounder shape to the bottom of his eyes and a sheen of green to his hair. "You aren't doing it for me either," I lie, but he steps in and kisses me.

"Fucking faggots!" Several rude masculine voices get our attention. A car has stopped, and the two guys inside are making hand gestures.

Haydar steps between us and the car and says something we can't hear. The passenger hits his buddy's head, and the car speeds off. "I don't hate being able to do that," Haydar admits when he turns around.

"Why do guys gotta be like that?" Eva demands as she walks off.

"Go after her," I tell Seb, who breaks into a jog to catch up.

I just walk along with Haydar for a few moments until I ask, "That was just some mortal guy thing you did, right?"

Haydar shakes his head, so I tug on his arm. He turns toward me and eases his glasses down enough for me to see the red ring around his pupils. "We're getting a full taste of these forms. Why not give them the full try?" he tells me with uncharacteristic confidence.

Why not indeed?

"What are you reading?" Uncle Delmar asks me two weeks later when I'm lounging on the sofa in the living room as he is heading out to work.

I hold up a mortal fashion magazine. I got it at a shop next to the coffee house where we four have been stopping for a cup and chat before catching the final bus home every Monday after school. This is the last week I'll be able to hang out as much, because prep for the term's play kicks into high gear on Friday with our first after-school meeting of the term, so I wanted Eva to help me find all the best magazines out there. She just reminded me that online is probably a better bet, but I pointed out that the mags were there and that online required a subscription I might not want next week.

"Okay, 'cause that makes sense," she told me, but she did grab three she said were still considered must-haves.

"Since when do you care so much about this … stuff?" my uncle chuckles.

I give him an annoyed look and pull the magazine back. "Since you're wearing a jacket and slacks that cannot possibly be in style, I wouldn't expect you to understand," I toss back.

He's silent for a second, then just claims, "These are classics; they don't go out of style."

I don't reply other than to roll my bright-blue eyes and flip the page with my pale fingers. That only draws his gaze, and he calls out as he heads toward the door, "Mother! Did you see that Blake is wearing makeup?"

I sit up and glare at his retreating figure. I freeze as Grandmother comes around the corner. We just look at each other. I can feel her gaze move from my lips, eyes, and even colored cheeks, and then travel down to the glitter polish on my fingernails. She just mutters something softly and goes back to her medications, which I bowed out of helping with. I had to do my nails, and it took time.

As this article right here by this world expert named Dr. Mavrel says, "Work what you have, because you won't have it for long." I'm just following a doctor's advice.

"Blake, how are you feeling about the term?" Counselor Mildford asks me the next afternoon during our weekly session.

I look up from my nails at the question. Normally she asks how this week's body is working out for me. I was about to say "great" because I was offered seats today on both the train and bus into campus. I was all prepared for more catcalls, but there's something about this body that was eliciting a different response from mortal men and boys. "This term? Don't you mean this new form?" I suggest, batting my eyelashes for emphasis.

The counselor's eyes widen, but she just rephrases her question. "Do you feel challenged or bored this term in any way?"

I shift in my seat and scrunch up this pale little nose I have as I make a face. "I'm doing fine in all my classes," I state plainly.

"Is that why your math instructor sent me a message that you failed the pop quiz today?"

I blink, and my mascaraed lashes suddenly feel heavy. I swallow, and I'm about to protest when I'm distracted by one of my painted nails as I raise my hands. I pause for just a second, then wave my hands in a dismissal. "It's just one quiz, plus who cares about maths?"

"I thought you did, since you've been in the advanced mortal courses and doing so very well in them."

We look at each other silently as I refuse to release the scream I'm holding inside. *I failed a pop quiz? In maths?* I've never failed a quiz, a paper, a test, or anything in school. That's the one place I could be better than normal and not be a freak.

"I'd like to give you a little pop quiz of my own," the counselor is now saying, and that breaks me out of my head.

"What?" I fall back now, my butt slipping against the seat instead of poised on the edge of the chair like the magazines showed.

"Just take this." She hands me what looks like a pair of lab goggles I've seen on old-time TV shows about high school kids in the mortal world. "You have to put them on, and then you'll see a series of dual images, one on each lens."

I look at the strap and complain, "This is gonna mess up my hair, and I spent a lot of time on it." Even more than when I'm trying to get my original hair to behave. I got up an hour early today to make this body look proper.

"Your hair will be fine, Blake. Put them on," Counselor Milford says in that same calm-but-demanding tone Grandmother uses, so I just do it.

There're a series of objects and people, the people shown only from the waist up. I sit through several displays, then I start to remove the goggles. "What am I supposed to be doing?" I reply when the counselor's hands on my mine prevent me from removing the goggles.

"Just look at them. You don't need to do anything other than try to relax and enjoy the show."

This isn't a show. A show would have a plot of some type or at least characters interacting with each other, but this is just objects and people. All different types of objects, all different types of people, though after a while I start to notice that the people seem to be my age or a bit older. Then I start to notice that the same objects are showing up multiple times, and some of the people appear to be the same, just with different clothing styles, clothing colors, or accessories. There had to be a trick to this, something I'm supposed to be doing, that a normal girl would be doing.

"That was great," Counselor Milford's voice interrupts my thoughts as the images fade to a single ocean view. "You may take them off now."

I carefully do so, but the band doesn't catch in my hair as expected. I pat the meticulously laid strands with my hands, but they seem to be just as I styled them. *Was it the styling gel I applied or something about the goggles themselves that prevented tangling?* I lean over and peer at them sitting on the desk just behind the counselor, but I don't see any electronic cord or attachment point.

"You can go to your next class, Blake. We're done for this afternoon."

I blink a few times, then stand up. "So, I'm fine just going early?"

"We're ending on time."

I get out my smartphone and check. That was the full period, as normal. I walk out but keep looking back at the goggles on the desk. *Did I fail that test, too?*

"Stop it!" Wigheard yells during drama club a week later. He's been working with the other actors on a tricky scene that involves several movements and complex dialogue exchanges. I'm trying to help with some detailed fittings on the other side of the stage.

Everyone gets quiet, and the professor floats up to the stage, saying, "What is going on?"

"I can hear that huffing and grumbling over here." Wigheard motions toward our costume and makeup team. "And it's distracting me. Us."

Nanuk sighs and gives me a glare. "We're just dealing with some difficulties. We can move our work backstage."

"You can't come back here!" the stage crew chief calls out. "Too much stuff around!"

"Why is someone being extra dramatic?" Professor Hermans asks as she turns toward our team.

The two others give me pointed looks, so I hold out my hands. "I don't think my current hands are designed to do this sort of work very well," I say in a lower voice. I'm in a female body this week, but my dark hair is buzzed, and I'm more rectangular shaped than the traditional teenage girl normally is. I've been living as butch as I can as a result, but you can't switch drama assignments once the show prep begins, or I'd be backstage or with lighting.

Nanuk rolls his eyes at my comment, but it's totally true that doing these tiny hand stitches is insane right now. The professor floats over to me and asks to look at my hands. As she examines them, she says, "Some of the best people with a needle and thread are male; these hands are as large as an adult man's. Have you been unable to do the work before today?"

I let Nanuk answer that for me, but I'm shocked when he says, "Blake tries, but honestly, I think stage craft is a better fit."

So that's why I've been through so many male and butch bodies and only one really feminine one? I feel my heart start to pound, and before I know what's happening, I'm on my back looking up at about a dozen faces staring down at me.

"I didn't see her disappear, right?" someone asks with a panicked edge to their voice.

"Victoria?" Professor Hermans calls out while Nanuk and Wigheard help me to my feet. I feel light-headed, which is just wrong in this body. I shake my head to clear it and feel the world spin around me. "Walk Blake to the clinic, please."

I let Victoria put her arm around me and lead me off the wings to the ramp. "Just one foot in front of the other," she tells me as we move.

I lean on her and blush as the scent of her perfume, soap, or whatever it is washes over me. "I can walk," I insist, but she never lets me go.

We don't end up in the school med office but outside the auditorium to sit at a picnic table. Victoria sits on the tabletop while I'm on the bench. Today she's in trousers, probably because as student director she's constantly running around between the professor, the stage, and all the departments. "Can you breathe calmly yet?" she asks me after a few minutes.

I nod silently. We sit like this until Victoria puts her face in her hands and lets out an intense sigh. "What's wrong?" I ask.

"I should ask you that, but I have a suspicion," she replies. "Blake, have you been trying to act like you think a person who looks like you currently do should?" I feel my mouth fall open, and my heart starts pounding again. "I'm not the only one noticing this, and you aren't the only one, by the way," she quickly adds.

"I, um, well, aren't we supposed to try these bodies out?"

"Yeah, you're trying them out to see if anything clicks with who you really are," she replies, repeating what our professor seems to be harping on every morning in class.

"Right! So I'm trying them out."

Victoria sighs again, then stands up and comes down to sit next to me. She faces me and puts on a tight smile. "In there ..." She motions toward the auditorium door we came out of. "... the actors use the costumes to help give life to the characters, but the characters aren't just the clothes or the accessories or even the dialogue. The characters aren't the actors, just a role they play."

I nod at this obvious statement.

Victoria looks at me then knits her brow. "You aren't getting this any more than Seb is, so I'm going to be more direct here. These bodies you're trying on aren't costumes. You're not supposed to be playing a role or becoming a character. They're an attempt to help you feel more yourself."

"Sure, yeah, which is why I'm trying different interests …"

"No. Just no. Be Blake. Keep doing everything you've done before."

Now I'm frowning. "That doesn't work! These bodies aren't … they don't … I don't sound like myself, let alone get up and down stairs the same way or have the same morning routine. I'm not really giving these a try if I don't adapt."

"Physical differences are real; they do require changes, but you as a person … you aren't this erratic. Just be as much of yourself as you can and stop acting."

I press my lips together. *Be myself.* A freak, an orphan, a migrant, a black girl or an Asian girl, or whatever. I don't know what I am. "I'm always playing a role," I let the words out softly.

Victoria hears them and leans to pull me into a hug. "That sucks, it really does. But just try to relax and see how being Blake works in each body. Please. I don't want you to become someone I can't be friends with when this is all done."

I clench my arms around her in fear at that sentence.

"To be blunt, the personalities you've been bouncing around with aren't at all attractive."

"Not even the fashionista?" I ask as we pull back from each other.

"That was slightly better than the goth jerk you were last week," she admits.

I wince at the memory of that. It was hard to be so emo with everyone last week and still try to salvage my coursework. "I'll try to just be me," I agree.

"Good, just try, and I'll call you on it if you start acting again," Victoria stipulates. She stands up and offers me a hand, helping me to my feet. "Let's get you to the clinic, then, so I don't get in trouble.

We've all reverted to our original forms Monday morning when the door to Russo's classroom opens and Counselor Milford walks in followed by several floating boxes. As the boxes move, I notice that the group of older students who have been helping out aren't there today. I've become so used to them that I'd assumed they would be there.

"Today we have a special guest whom you all should have met at least once," the professor announces. "We've been noticing in your discussions and journals, as well as through reports from older students, as well as your teachers, that many of you are struggling to live in the revolving body situation. This week, we're going to slow down and adjust our course to reflect some realities we hadn't considered."

Tutor Lubit is helping the counselor hand out the same goggles I used in her office two weeks ago. Each student gets a pair and looks at it. Brizo holds them up to her eyes and looks through them at me but doesn't actually slip them onto her head. I glare down at mine. *This again?* The counselor's questions and statements have been different since I used these before, but I don't see why I need to go through all of this again.

"Hello, everyone!" the counselor says brightly. "I'm going to say the spell, and you'll repeat it while your fingertips are pressed against these two little green spots on the sides of the goggles." *I didn't do that, so is that why I need to do it again?*

We all copy her and then place them on our heads. The parade of paired images streams over my field of vision. This time I try to simply watch and not think about how I'm supposed to act or what I'm supposed to do.

"Very good, just keep watching, and be silent unless you really need to say something," I hear Milford's voice say farther from me.

After a while, we get the command to remove them and place them back into the boxes that are floating in the aisles and stopping by the desks.

Milford is still at the front of the room while Lubit is directing the boxes out of our classroom. Professor Russo puts up the display about gender that we went over the first week after Solstice. "Let's review the differences between gender, reproductive sex, and sexual orientation today. We're going to look at the issue of stereotypes from the mortal realm versus the enchanted one. Counselor Milford, would you help me out?"

"Of course, Professor. Let's start with you all telling me what the definitions are for these terms."

Several hands go up, but I keep my down. I thought I knew these, but maybe I really don't, so I get ready to listen before I make any notes.

The definitions range from the standard mortal ones to the mage ones. Then the counselor flips our world. "Are any of these objective definitions?"

No one raises a hand for several seconds. Even Haydar and Maxima are unusually silent.

"Brains develop shortcuts to help speed up the processing of information," Professor Russo jumps in to tell us. *Was there something like that in our textbook?* I can't recall a chapter or page, but it seems familiar. "The shortcuts by their very function distort reality. Stereotypes are a sort of cultural shortcut that is partly created by our minds, but which are primarily taught over generations. For all of you raised in and primarily living in the mortal world, this means you may have a lot of those shortcuts in your heads. When you look in your mirrors after our transformations, you start consciously or subconsciously behaving in a way you think is appropriate for a person like that to behave. That is not the goal of this class."

I hear mutters around me from the other students. *I'm not the only one who's been playing a role then.*

"I got the analysis of the goggle test back. This was gauging your responses to gender, racial, age, ethnicity, and other stereotypes drawn from similar mortal psychological tests. Your collective results show a high rate of internalized mortal stereotypes," Milford tells us. The display at the front of the classroom shows a graph of gender, sex, race, and several other categories of stereotypes.

I see a hand shoot up and turn to see Haydar raise to speak. "Does this mean the final spell won't work?" That gets a loud reaction that the Professor has to curb by tapping her desk with her pointer several times.

"No, it just means that we have to help you all, and you have to help each other be more aware of when your behavior is changing to reflect a stereotype instead of yourself."

"But if we're in a different body, that does affect behavior," counters Oswine, our resident sport star. He grumbles when he's told to raise his hand first. He stands up when recognized and repeats the statement, adding,

"Bodies are different. Last week I couldn't do some of the moves that came easily to me on the court or the field."

"No one is saying that bodies don't matter," Professor Russo states. Milford nods but stays quiet. I've been watching carefully, but she never signals me out for attention, so I'm trying to accept what they're telling us. "Think about trans folk in the mortal world, or anyone who simply doesn't fit into the ideals of what someone in their particular group is supposed to be like. Bodies don't always enhance who we are—sometimes they challenge it. This class is designed to help you become more aligned between body and personality, between matter and spirit, even."

I glance around casually but find every student as focused as I'm trying to be.

"This alignment is important for mages because magic is a matter of balance. Every word, gesture, tone— even thought—can impact what we do. When we as a people figured that out, our lives and our lifespans improved greatly."

We must be in balance; that's what our teacher is telling us. I've never felt in balance my entire life. I'm shocked and then relieved when Brizo whispers, "I'm so many different things; how do I find that balance?"

I reach over and lay my hand palm up on the space between our desks. In a moment, Brizo takes my hand and gives it a squeeze. I look to see Eva, Seb, and Haydar looking at me; I see other study buddy groups also exchanging looks. None of us are in this alone.

Epilogue: You are You

Dear Journal,

A week in our original forms, and then the final spell.

I knew what I wanted at the start of the term; I knew what I wanted for years. Now I don't know. Wigheard and most of the others like me say that they didn't change. If I change, will I be glad or not?

Will I finally be in balance and be my true self?

Or will the Fates force me to learn to be someone else?

I'm working myself up again, and I need to calm down for final exams before the big day.

I've gotten my maths scores back on track and the rest of my classes are going well. The spring play went well, and Professor Hermans was so happy that she gave us all tickets to the opening week of her off-Broadway show that starts this summer.

I close my journal and try to get some studying done, but I just can't. I leave my room and go to the dining room where Grandmother is watching a video on the tablet my uncle and I gave her recently. She shows me the live stream from a flower show happening right now in the enchanted realm; she didn't go, even though I know she'd have loved to. "I didn't know you were busy," I start to excuse myself, but she just turns the tablet face down and nods toward another spot at the table.

Once I've seated myself, the trays of biscuits and lemonade float out of the kitchen to settle between us on the table. "Did you know I was coming out to talk to you?"

"I hoped you might," she replies as she takes one of the soft treats and one of the crisp ones and places them on a small plate. We stay still until the drinks are poured, then she says, "You'll always be my Blake. I will always love you."

I feel the tears at the edges of my eyes, so I wipe them with the back of my hands. "That's what I needed to hear, Grandma," I sob.

Then she's on my side of the table, her arms around me, and we're both crying.

When we've separated again and enjoyed a biscuit or two, she tells me something else. "Delmar has made sure to take next week off work. We were thinking of a holiday after the final spell. Perhaps to the enchanted realm, or back to London. We can do both if you like."

"Can I decide that later? I think I'm ready, but ..."

Grandmother reaches out and pats my hand. "That's a benefit of magic: we can change travel plans so easily." We both chuckle.

"I've been so busy with classes and all this figuring-out-what-I-am stuff that I haven't been much help. I'm sorry," I say.

"This hasn't even been a full year of your life; you can help me this summer if you want," she offers. At my nod she takes another biscuit from the tray and puts it on my plate. "Let me tell you, though, that we're in for a rainy summer if my herbs are right, and they always are."

I relax, listening to her talk to me about her work and patients in both realms.

Today is our last day of *True You*. Haydar, Eva, Seb, and I are standing in our clique. There is a floating four-sided mirror between us, but we can easily see each other around the sides of it.

Tutor Lubit is going to each team and checking in with them, but he pauses when he gets to us. "Blake, we'll need to remove the dampener. May I?" he asks.

I suck in a breath, then let it go, nod, and hold out my wrist, noting that my teammates move a little closer to me. "We're right here; we're all gonna be right here," Seb says. Eva and Haydar echo his words, and the tutor nods as he makes the correct gestures and touches the bracelet.

I feel a rush of power through my body, but I take deep breaths as Counselor Milford taught me. I smile at the trio and give the tutor a nod. "Very good," he tells me before turning to join the professor.

"Everyone ready?" Professor Russo asks our class. For this one meeting we've taken over the gym, and the classes that should be in here are outside. Only the older students who have been helping are on the main floor with us, though off to one side in a warded section. Any members of our immediate families are in the stands behind warded screens that still allow them to watch us. I look up and nod at my uncle and grandmother.

All of us prick a finger and repeat the words of the last spell we'll cast in *True You 101*. The air changes around me, lines of fire race up and down every part of my body, and I close my eyes. When I open them, I look at my friends' new selves first.

Haydar's hair is straighter, his eyes a bit wider, and his skin a touch darker, but he still wears his glasses. He might be a bit broader across the chest, but otherwise, he looks like the same geek I've gotten to know over these past months as we walk home together. "Hey, I look more like my father now," he laughs as he touches his cheeks and pushes up his frames.

Eva's chest is less pronounced, her teeth are straighter, and her skin has lightened even more, but she still has her fiery hair whose curls will freak in humidity.

She looks like the Eva who has become my good friend these past several months as we've shared supplies in the bathroom and chatted on the ride home many nights. "I was worried about this," she says, motioning to her chest, "but now that I think about it, it'll make cheering easier and probably help me as a reporter, because I'll be taken more seriously."

"That's one way to deal with sexism," I joke, squeezing her hand. She laughs.

Seb's hair is lighter and his eyes bluer, even though his skin is a shade or two darker. His height and bulk haven't changed. "Still team manager for me, then," he chuckles.

"Cheer squad could use more guys," Eva tosses out, but he only makes a face. We all laugh at that for a few moments. He'll figure out what his mundane skills and mage gifts are next year when we all take *Your Talents* both terms. Right now we just look at each other and grin until I notice he isn't the only one staring at me.

Eva motions to the mirror. I look and see me, Blake, exactly as I was before. I run through a checklist of what my body feels like and find it all as it was at the start of the term. No, that's not quite true. I can feel my smile deep down in every part of me as I squeeze Eva's and Haydar's hands.

"Hey, our parents are coming!" someone yells out, and soon all of us have turned toward the descending horde.

I lean into the crook of Seb's arm, and he gives me a gentle hug. Before I can ask if this is okay with him, Victoria's voice rings out. "Thank goodness that tension is over with now." Victoria tilts her head to one side and shakes it at us with a huge grin.

The junior and senior classes have come into the gym as well. Between them and our parents, there is a stream of people's hands to shake or hugs to exchange as we are welcomed as we really are. Wigheard, Nima, and Su-Bin head in our direction. They each look me over and ask without words if I've changed by scanning my midsection for a few seconds too long. "I'm still intersex," I bluntly state, but in a hushed tone.

"That will make the magic courses more fun next term," Su-Bin replies with a blush. I want to ask what they mean, but I see my family coming over quickly.

"My Blake," Uncle says as he holds out his arms for a hug. I accept it and then give a hug to my grandmother.

I shake hands with Seb's parents and nod at his younger brother, who quickly becomes a non-stop fount of questions. I note that the Hileses glance at each other a few times as they look at my uncle, their eyes a bit sad. Questions about my uncle and my parents haven't gone away since I shifted dimensions, but I've been so focused on how I've been changing and what I'd become that I've almost forgotten.

"Blake, how shall we refer to you now, in terms of pronouns?" Madame Hiles asks me, and everyone in our two families looks at me.

That's one I hadn't really thought about this entire school year, because I'd always assumed my body would change and it would be obvious. I feel the correctness of the words as they pass my lips, "I think 'they' and 'them' work best, because I may change from one day to another."

"Can I just call you my lover then?" Seb teases.

"Does that mean you're having sex?" the youngest Hiles asks. Victoria puts her hands over his ears while their parents and my grandmother and uncle all start talking extra loudly about vacations.

I let Seb lead me a couple of steps away. "I'm mostly just me too," he points out with a shrug.

"I'll put up with mostly you then for a while longer," I tease back.

"Don't even," Victoria's voice interrupts us before we can get any closer. She's doing such a great job of keeping the youngest under control that the two Hiles boys are lovingly taunting each other. I look back over the gym and see everyone accepting all of us for who we are— even Burim, who is currently chatting with the Institution's head of girls' sport.

I let my gaze go back to my family, now talking with Brizo's mother. I haven't forgotten. Questions about my family's mysterious past can wait since I've had them for over a decade. But the new Blake Trudeau won't just let those questions go unanswered. If anything, turning out to have been my true self all along has made me more confident than ever that I will uncover the truth. The look my grandmother gives me lets me know she realizes as much.

Since 1995, TJ Eckhart's fiction and non-fiction work has been challenging readers to look at themselves and their world through a different lens. *True You 101* continues Eckhart's challenge to reimagine a magic world colliding with the mortal one in regard to our true nature, one that rejects either a reversal or continuation of our everyday biases in favor of the more realistic complexities of what such a realm might be like. If you're willing to risk opening up your mind, you may find Eckhart's worlds opening up your heart as well.

You may find her at her main <u>website</u> or join her adventures on <u>Patreon</u>